No Black in the Rainbow

By Lawrence Gayle

DORRANCE PUBLISHING CO
EST. 1920
PITTSBURGH, PENNSYLVANIA 15238

Dorrance Publishing Co
585 Alpha Drive
Pittsburgh, PA 15238
Visit our website at *www.dorrancebookstore.com*

ISBN: 979-8-88729-085-0
eISBN: 979-8-88729-585-5

The silence was eerie, but it told Cane that he was on the right track. After all this was a semi-jungle and one should hear jungle sounds. However, over the last few days in tracking the "Maubino Mauchetes," Cane knew that the absence of sound was an indication that he and his men were not far behind them. Their name loosely translated meant "blood only of the family." A splinter guerrilla group consisting usually of about eight to twelve of the Biafraian Army (BA) fighters, they use machetes or long knives to do their killing. And killed they did. Village after village the truncated remains of what was once humans could be seen strewn all over and the scavengers would feast. In fact, Cane used the circling of vultures above as a sort of guide as to where he should head or to pick up their trail. He would see them circling like planes in a holding pattern from the control tower, then the lowest would drop as it saw available booty. He was in the jungle just over a week now. They had not encountered any Maubinos but had seen their handy disgusting work in the last village; guided to this last village massacre by the unofficial aviary spotters. His tracker had picked up their trail, and he estimated that they were only a few hours behind this particular group of dohyas slaughterers.

(That particular name was given to anyone who was beneath total and absolute contempt by their fellow man.) If you were called so in public, it was fighting talk.

Cane kept scanning the skies, looking to see if any fresh "circling" was taking place. There was none. Based on the terrain, the personnel carrier would not be able to navigate to the next area highlighted on his map, so Cane told two of his men to head for the area and he would link up with them there.

If you were not of the Maubinos ethnic group, absolutely nothing would save you from the savagery that they perpetrated; neither men, women, nor children were spared. Basically, the number of ethnic groups were hard to define as the mixture comprised of a variety of inter bonding. However, there were four large groups, mainly the Igbos, Yorba, Fulare, and Hauser. The war caused other smaller groups to take sides with larger groups for protection and sustenance.

Why…why…? Cane thought to himself, but the answer was always there. Tribes have been fighting tribes since time immortal; the cavemen drawings were a testament to that. All over the world man would kill his fellow man because of race or creed. Later on, in time, the killing was justified for political or religious beliefs. Cane could not help a deep sight as he led the ten federal troops and the two Biafraian corporals out of the dense bush. The irony of the situation was that they were trying to catch up with the Maubinos; not to engage them but to let them know that the Civil War was over.

They finally came to the village highlighted on the map. It consisted of about fifteen to twenty abodes formed in a semi-circle; and from their vantage point it looked completely deserted. Cane thought this scenario was one of two things: either the villagers had scattered once they got a hint the Maubinos were in the area, or the Maubys were already there hiding as they knew a patrol was on their trail and possibly set up an ambush. Only Cane was armed with a sub-machine gun, the Uzi 406; the rest of the federal solders had British single shot AR20 repeating rifles. These were good to pick off the enemy at short distances, but if a Maubino charged you out of the bush with a glistening machete raised, the Uzi could unload a magazine in the blink of an eye, which was your best bet in surviving.

Cane surveyed the compound again and again with his Regal B405 power scope. Nothing. The eerie silence prevailed, and he knew that the Maubinos were still there; although there were no bodies to be seen, or vultures circling. They were tracking this particular group since they encountered the last carnage.

This was the closest Cane had come to actually encountering them. He felt a rush of adrenaline as he briefed the men of their modus operandi.

Hand signals confirmed that everything was as planned, and they walked guarded into the compound. The two Biafraian corporals had megaphones and they began to repeat that the war was over in different dialects as they cautiously approached the center of the compound. Nothing or no one stirred. "You will not be harmed," the corporals bellowed over and over again. "Just come out and be recognized."

Cane had circled the first abode to his right and came up very quietly from the rear. He peeped through the low window and nearly choked at the sight before him.

A Maubino guerrilla had a girl, she could not be more than twelve, on a low table stark naked. With a patrol arriving at any time, this piece of crap wanted to satisfy his lust first. Her hint of breasts was just budding, and there was no arm hair as she covered her eyes in anticipation of the horror that was about to befall her. The guerrilla had his pants down by his ankle; one hand held her across her stomach, her legs forced upon his shoulders and his back was arched as he steadied his manhood, which was huge, for that first ripping thrust. It would be like a cannon fired into a papier-mâché dwelling. Ripped total apart.

Cane took in all this in a millisecond. "Stop," he bellowed, cocking the Uzi. The man, in even a briefer millisecond, had the girl in front of him in a choke hold and his machete in the other hand as he sprung around from where the order of stop had come. "Let her go and listen," Cane said. They could still hear the announcements by the megaphones. Cane hoped that this man spoke one of the dialects or at least English.

"Put down your gun and back away or I will kill her," the guerrilla said as he inched the machete closer to the throat. The girl's eyes were now popping out, and any second now Cane expected them to really fall out. Cane relaxed his breathing. He did speak very good English; the missionaries that were a part of everyday life before war broke out had done a good job in that respect, Cane thought. He refocused now; Cane could see that there were bundles of humanity huddled in the far corner of the room, another Maubino stood guard over them with his machete raised.

"Listen, there is no way I am going to put down my gun. The war is over, listen to your own guys."

The guerrilla did not even seem to be aware of the megaphone messages;

he inched the machete a little deeper into the flesh of the girl. "Drop the gun or I kill her," he yelled almost hysterically and jerked the girl further up his body.

"If you kill her, then make peace with your maker as this will be your last day on earth, you piece of crap. You would kill her after you had satisfied your lust and chop her up for the scavengers, so go ahead, do your thing, the war is over, and you want to die. I have forty bullets with your name on them and that of your comrade over there, so go ahead." His voice was clear, and he enunciated each word deliberately. As he spoke, he waved the Uzi menacingly from one to the other Maubino. Cane was not certain if one of the megaphone message had gotten through or the firm way he held the Uzi had an impact, but he let go of the girl, dropped the machete, and pulled up his pants. In an effort to do things quickly, he had caught his manhood, which had gone flaccid, in his zipper; as he pulled up, he let out a short-lived, agonizing scream. Cane could not help but smile when he saw what had happened.

As he rounded the abode with the guerrilla, Uzi still held firm, he saw that other Maubinos were exiting from other dwellings with their machetes held by the blade. There were eleven of them in total. Technically, they were not prisoners of war…. Cane felt the anger start to rise again in his stomach as they could not even be charged for anything unless a villager from a previous village had escaped and witnessed the carnage they perpetrated on that particular village and was willing to testify to those facts; there was nothing one could do. They were instructed to pile their machetes in the middle of the compound. The eleven of them would be taken back to headquarters and be processed, whatever that meant. Cane ordered the NFA soldiers to check every abode to make sure all was well. He wondered how many young girls were raped and tortured by this group before they arrived, and even more so how many had been killed. Cane hoped the time lapse was too short as they were aware that NFA patrol was close by. The NFA sergeant reported that there were no deaths or casualties and they had completed their search. Cane made a heavy sigh and gave thanks to an unseen god.

Villagers started to emerge from their homes, and in a short time about forty of them had gathered around. Apparently, a look-out for the Maubinos had informed their leader that NFA patrol of about ten men was closing in. Rather than scatter and be picked off one by one, because they did not know the war was over, they figured that they had an advantage if they hid and ambushed their pursuers. Close-quarters fighting with the machete/knife would be more effective than a rifle. The villagers were threatened with immediate death if they made a sound, and so positions were taken up. Except for the piece of crap Cane had stopped that wanted to satisfy his lust before any fighting took place. Had they not arrived when they did, he was certain rape and slaughter would have taken place.

Cane discovered two things: everyone in the compound spoke English, including the Maubinos, as well as their native dialect, and the caught-his-penis-in-his-zipper guy was the Maubinos' leader. Cane had nothing but contempt for him and wondered how many young girls he had raped and slaughtered since the beginning of the war. He could feel the bile building up in his stomach and the inner rage that burned as the flooded of brutal images over the last few days enveloped his consciousness and threatened to explode with a burst of his Uzi on the men who called themselves...soldiers. The brutality was on both sides; the NFA also had its splinter groups who dealt out their own gruesome justice whenever they came up on non-ethnic persons. Although he could not really condone their actions, their justification for such action was based on retaliation for the brutality exercised by the BA groups. Most NFA soldiers had joined the army long before the outbreak of civil war, and so many ethnic groups were banned together. Some had deserted to become BA as they were of that ethnic group. Consequently, the regular NFA soldier was not so prone to the merciless and wanton killing like the BA groups. The NFA groups were more into raping the women and burning villages. Many BA soldiers were conscripted or formed their own militia with their leader taking orders from a central command.

Just as he was about to radio for transport to meet him at a designated point, he felt a slight tug on his shirt. It was the about-to-be-raped little girl. Her eyes were naturally wide but seemed so much softer as she thanked him and gave him what appeared to be an animal tooth through which a leather strap was attached. He took it and held her by her thin, slender shoulders for a long time, staring into her eyes. "This is to keep you safe for always," she said softly. She was indeed twelve, and he could not help but wonder in ten years where she would be, what would she make of her life, and also the countless thousands of children that this war had affected. Cane was glad that this was his last "find and inform" operation. He was also glad that it was only after the official declaration to end hostilities by the Biafraian leader Maj. Gen Effiong that he had actually gone on patrol in what could be described as a "mop up" operation as the likelihood of a major encounter with any Biafraian army unit was remote. His main occupation during the war was centered on training and logistics. At least Maj. Gen Effiong was able to get in touch with mainstream army units to let them know that an official surrender was in place. Gen Ojukwu, the Biafraian head and his family had sought asylum in another African state and left Effiong to talk terms as head of the army.

If the BA had the resources that the Nigerian Federal Army (NFA) had, this civil war would have been over a long time ago. One item which beset the BA was a lack of communication equipment. Time and time again they had to use runners to get orders from the field headquarters to commanders further ahead or guarding their flank. Even times when they had some equipment, inexperienced operators would convey garbled messages, which led to troops heading the wrong way or closing in their own soldiers. "Roger," "Ten-Four," "Over" were loosely used in the middle of an order or sentence, thus making precise instructions difficult to understand. Notwithstanding their drawbacks, from intelligence reports the BA soldiers were formidable fighters. Time and time again they had withstood vaunted aggression and then counterattacked the more resourceful NFA soldiers. The NFA, which had equipment and resources, failed to capitalize on their advantage. Cane vividly remembered in July 1968, when an elite Biafraian platoon was on the retreat to Enugu, their home base, soldiers were inflicting wounds on themselves as they retreated so as to win sympathy from the populous as brave and dedicated soldiers in the fight for their freedom. If the NFA had suitable intelligence information and army leaders who understood logistics, Enugu could have easily been taken and the war would be short lived, as Enugu was the heart of the BA effort.

There were several official NFA splinter groups operating in the Mid-Eastern section, and Cane's group was but one of them. He traveled with two BA corporals so that when they encountered these BA splinter groups, the corporals could convey to the Maubinos or others in whatever dialect was used, that the war was over.

The personnel carrier was right on schedule, and as they journeyed back to field headquarters, Thomas Alexander Cane could not help wandering what was he doing in the middle of a civil war; granted now ended. His thoughts were rudely interrupted by the pop-pop sound of several AK-47s as it ripped into the army vehicle. Cane was out in a flash, sprayed a short burst in the direction of the incoming burst as he hit the ground and rolled under the truck. He looked up to see Corporal Bosun with the megaphone beside him. Cane was not sure who was firing, a nervous FNA or BA army unit. Friendly fire was a part of this horrible civil war. Cane reasoned that it would be more likely a BA unit as some of their solders carried AK-47s, and their exit muzzle sound was unmistakable. He instructed Corporal Bosun to use the megaphone to announce that the war was over. Apparently, the announcement got above the gunfire, and there was a lull in the shooting. Corporal Cheke joined in the announcements from under the army vehicle, and the silence persisted. Cane grabbed the megaphone and identified his unit and their purpose; he spoke in the dialect of the Igbos, which made up the majority of the BA army. Even legitimate BA army units once separated from their headquarters by long distance had trouble in communications. Since Christmas was not a big, celebrated holiday here, only frontline units knew of the cease fire and surrender; so fighting persisted well into the end of December. Runners were still trying to reach outlaying units, as Cane and his patrol were doing.

Caught-his-penis-in-his-zipper surfaced and spoke in several dialects as the silence continued. Finally, seven BA army soldiers emerged, three from one side and four from the other. In the exchange of gunfire, incredibly, no one was hit. Cane could not help but wonder who had given the order to conduct an ambush at this particular point. One hundred meters down the road would have been ideal as the ambushers would have a high ground; shooting down at the vehicle. As it was now, the vehicle had the high road and they attacked from below, making it difficult to hit anyone who had taken refuge under the truck. To shoot anyone, they had to stand up in the ditch, making them easier target to counter fire. They all piled into the truck, and once more they were on their way. Cane hope to reach headquarters without further incident. How many had died in wars throughout history after a cease fire/surrender had taken place? He lulled back into elusive rest, which was denied to him over the last few days. He pondered on the events that had gotten him into this situation.

Military adviser to the NFA with the rank of Captain was his official title.

In the first year of the war, his training at Sandhurst paid dividends. He felt a sense of considerable ease knowing that the whole NFA solders were equipped with Enfield No4 MK1. The British Government was glad to unload so many thousands of rifles at one go, practically clearing out their entire stock. This facilitated easy interchange of parts and ammo. From intelligence gathered, the BA was supplied by a matrix of suppliers, making it difficult for logistics management. It was not unusual in a unit of, say, twenty men they all had different weapons. So called friends of Biafra were only too glad to unload their antique store of weapons to them at tremendous cost. The BA also had foreign mercenaries fighting for them, and of course, they were the best equipped.

Someone in the BA had taken stock (perhaps a Sandhurst graduate) and realized that they had to rationalize, and in short while, AK-47s became standard issue for the more frontline soldiers and for all officers.

The truck bump and grinned its way along the rough road, and Cane reflected on his life once more.

Kingston, Jamaica 1957–1961

Born in Kingston, Jamaica, on June 10th, 1940, of a middle-class family, his mother died when he was two and it was his fathers' mother who raised him. He rarely saw his father who was always busy in politics. At a very early age, his grandmother realized that she had an exceptional grandchild. She could never forget the day when at age four he came running into the house shouting, "Grandma…Grandma, there are a number of felines in the yard." *Felines in the yard?* she pondered, *Oh, cats…. Where did this child pick up that meaning?* She knew that at four he read the daily newspaper flawlessly, but felines? It was right then she decided, after informing his father, that she would have him tested to see if her hunch was right. A few weeks later, she was sitting in the foyer of Fitz-Henlys Institute for the for the Gifted while young Cane was whisked away to be tested. The minutes ticked into two hours until she saw a beaming Mrs. Isabella Fitzhenly coming towards her, with Cane happily skipping as he sucked on a popsicle. She was asked to come into the inner office and ushered into a more comfortable and luxurious chair than was in the foyer.

"Mrs. Cane, you have an exceptional child; he has aced every possible test we had for his age group in half the time…."

Grandma Cane beamed as Mrs. Fitz-Henly continued to shower praise upon praise on her grandson. She was completely lost in thought and only became conscious when she heard, "a special school."

"Yes, Mrs. Cane," continued Ms. Fitzhenly, "young Cane should be enrolled here immediately. As you know, this is a boarding school, and I am pleased to say we would offer him a completely full scholarship in all aspects of his stay." Grandma Cane was flabbergasted; she did not expect events to unfold so quickly.

Once she got a word in edgewise, she explained that she would have to consult his father and would get back to her as soon as possible. She made her excuse and departed the building with young Cane still happily sucking on another popsicle…. Where did he get it from? Cane's father was also delighted, and young Cane was shipped off to the FHIG at the beginning of the new term. Having Cane at the Institute on a scholarship was a win-win situation for the Institute as whenever their charges competed against other schools of the same caliber, the winning school got regional and sometimes international recognition.

The FHIG was a large u-shaped two-story building with classrooms, canteen, and recreation rooms on the ground floor and dorms on the upper. The dorms were further subdivided into sections, with each section having a male or female "dorm warden" person, depending on the age group and gender in that dorm. There were about forty-five students ranging from ages six to eleven, almost equally divided by gender. As he advanced in age, he continued to amaze his fellow students and visiting teachers with his uncanny ability to solve all things in science and mathematics that were appropriate for his age and just beyond. Gifted and/or acoustic students tend to excel in various fields, mathematics, science, language, etc. Cane was uniquely blessed that he could learn a language very quickly on hearing it for the first time.

Frequent visits from his grandmother helped foster a close-knit bond with her. It was therefore a shock to her when at eighteen and just graduated from FSG, he chose to become a cadet in the Royal Fusiliers. He had never hinted to her that the army was of paramount consideration in his future. The Fusiliers was an elite branch of the British Army, and a unit was stationed in Jamaica at the time. With so many British territories this side of the world, Jamaica was the ideal launching site to cover territories in Central America, the Caribbean, and South America. His decision was based on the fact that in the future he would be an officer in an elite army unit. His father, after weighing the pros and cons and convinced of his son's own unshaken desire, okayed his application to join the army.

The Royal Fusiliers comprise of ninety percent English Officers and Cadets and ten percent of other Commonwealth countries cadets. No officers. Cane would be the first Jamaican to be specifically accepted for the Fusiliers, and that was because he had excelled in every physical and aptitude test they gave him. As a young man, Cane was an avid reader of everything Ian Fleming wrote. He imagined that with scholastic success and training he would be attain some of the deeds attributed to the fictional character James Bond.

He was still eighteen, so he knew that he had to undergo basic training for three years before he was eligible at twenty-one to go the England and enter Sandhurst Military Academy. Sandhurst was the equivalent to West Point in America. Young army cadets from all over the British Commonwealth were sent to Sandhurst to be trained as future leaders of their respective country's armies. Since the sun never sets on the British Commonwealth, one can only imagine the multi-ethnic potpourri that existed there.

Basic training was brutal and demanding. Of the forty-two cadets who started, only thirty-one remained after six months, and the final count at the end of the three year was thirty. As he did during his high school tenure, he excelled in everything mental and the physical aspect of the course. He was a very popular cadet, and his grandmother's goodies, which she brought very often, highlighted his personality even more as he shared with his fellow cadets. He graduated as an

Officer-Cadet First Class with commendation in every field. Two days after graduation, he was ordered to the office of Field Marshall, R.F. Coker (all his other distinguish titles and medals would take pages...suffice to say he was well decorated).

It came as no surprise to him when he was told that he had been accepted to the Sandhurst Military Academy. He knew of other young Jamaicans who had distinguish themselves at Sandhurst, but he knew he was the first to opt to join the Fusiliers. What came as a surprise to him was the information that he should report there within three days of the new term, beginning on September 25th, 1961. He should make all travel arrangements and pass them on to his Captain. Cane was ecstatic. This was the end of August, so he had a couple of weeks to "chill out" so to speak.

Obtaining a two-week pass was a cinch, and he went straight to his grandmother's home. Those two last weeks with her were very enjoyable. She catered to his every need, and he basked in the attention. After three years at army camp, he indulged himself to the fullest. A young lady named Opal Reid, whom his grandmother had brought to the army base on several occasions, frequented the house in those two weeks. He soon discovered that his grandmother had hopes of him forming some bond with her. She was always commenting on how Opal is this and Opal is that, her family is this and her family is that. No opportunity was spared in his presence to extol the virtues of the Reid family and their daughter. Opal was not a stunning beauty, neither was she unattractive. During her visits to the army base, they had gone for long walks and even French kissed several times. Cane had lost his virginity at the FSFG on several occasions as he and other young men devise ways to get into the girls' dorm undetected. Sex with Opal to him was a youthful exercise that young men his age should indulge. There were no religious recrimination nor constraints. Once there was privacy and kissing started, it seemed natural to consummate the relationship that way instead of suppressing the need to do so. There were no special odors or behavior to guide the human male when the female was ready for sex; arousal for both was hard to contain once a certain level of intimacy was reached. Their lovemaking was sometimes leisurely and other times hurried. The prospect of pregnancy was negated as she told him at the onset that she took the pill to regulate her menstrual flow. Nothing was said about love or that she would be waiting for him. As soon as the subject of their relationship cropped up during those intimate times, Cane would point out that he was going away for four years and would prefer to see what developed rather than make any promise. His father, who by now was very active in politics, came to see him the day before his departure. The meeting was cordial, like strangers bidding goodbye rather than father and son. Cane had not expected any gushing superlatives or manly advice, and he was not disappointed. After a short while, his father made his excuse and left. His goodbye to Opal; that night was a repetition earlier sexual encounters. **England 1962–1966.**

His flight from Kingston to London Heathrow by British Overseas Airway Corporation (BOAC) was uneventful. Touchdown was in the early morning. As the pilot steadied on his flight path in, Cane got a glimpse of the "mother country." Houses were built in a continuous row along well-groomed and clean avenues. Except for the gates to each house and chimney stacks, from above they appeared as one continuous barrack. There were many vehicles of different sizes whizzing along highways. The verdant green of the land was awe inspiring. The jolt of wheels in contact with the tarmac told him they had touchdown safely and he listened as the retro engine was deployed. As they taxied across what seemed like endless spaces to their designated gate, Cane could see at ground level that this was indeed a green and fertile land. It was mid-September, and along borders he could see a variety of blooming flowers everywhere. As they disembarked and entered the terminal building, he was approached by an army officer who introduced himself as Lt. Colonel Harold Jones and he was the chief liaison at Sandhurst. He was hustled through Immigration to a waiting car. This was his first journey outside of Jamaica, and also his first long distant flight. He did not count the few helicopter flights from one base camp to another in Jamaica. He hardly spoke as they weaved in and out of traffic and made their way to the motorway from Heathrow to London. Cane hardly spoke, taking in the wonderful sights that unfolded before him. As they drove through London, he was further amazed at the architecture of the buildings. Lt. Jones could see that he was impressed and would call out from time to time points of interest as they drove by it. By the time they exited the suburbs of London and were making their way, Cane realized that the temperature was slightly warmer the more miles added. He asked Lt. Jones to explain. Lt. Jones agreed and said as the Academy was in the South of England, and although it was late September, they were having unusually warm weather and they tend to have a warmer climate than say London. The rest of the journey was done in silence as the countryside whizzed pass, and Cane continued to soak up his new surroundings.

Turning into the main gate of the Academy, Cane became even more impressed with this soon-to-be-his new home. It was magnificent, so well laid out, and the buildings seem to gleam. Lt. Jones took him to a dorm, spoke to someone while he hovered in the background and informed him that he was in C block, dorm room was 5b bed/locker 3, and pointed him the direction. "Be up by five-thirty a.m. and be ready to meet the Commander by six a.m.," were his parting words. Cane entered the dorm, which housed six cot-like beds and a upright locker with a table attached. A lamp was also affixed to the table. There were three other cadets unpacking, and they all looked up as he entered. An Indian and two whites. As he found his bunk, another Indian entered. A sort of awkward silence developed, and as Cane rested his suitcase, he exclaimed, "My name is Thomas Cane and I am from Jamaica."

The Indian beside him said, "I am Seri Maros Batlavala and I am from Bombay in India." The silence was broken, and all began to introduce themselves to each other. Dorm 5 was made up of two Jamaicans, two Indians, and two Australian cadets. Cane did not recognize the other Jamaican, who was about two years his senior. He found out later that Delroy Black had come to attend Sandhurst two years ago and had fallen ill with some unknown virus. It took almost fourteen months for him to fully recover, hence his late arrival to Sandhurst. Needless to say Cane and himself became bosom buddies. Before they knew it, the casual chatter among them lasted until "lights out." Cane reckoned that he had just close his eyes, when the blast of the roll call bugle awakened him. All the other cadets were up, and an air of urgency prevailed as they hit the showers and readied themselves for roll call by six a.m. In the quadrant before each housing unit A-C, about thirty cadets lined up in military style and stood to attention under the direction of the unit captain. (Cane imagined that each cadet had gotten their get-acquainted-to Sandhurst-packet as he did and knew exactly what to do and what procedure to follow.)

The commandant of Sadhurst…B.A. Wakeford (with a string of

alphabet letters grouped in fours after his name and enough medals on his chest to cause some discomfort) took a podium and introduced himself. He outlined the basic rules and regulations and wished them all Godspeed, and they were dismissed for breakfast.

The next few days became routine as each cadet found their particular niche in what they excelled at between studies and the physical aspect of training. Cane applied himself in all courses, and it was no surprise that he mastered all of them with distinction. He especially liked unarmed combat, and on his days off, would travel to Camberley, a local town a couple of miles away, to a Tae-Kwan-do dojo to further enhance his skills. In the four years at Sandhurst and doing karate, he became a black belt. His dojo master at the mini-installation ceremony of his black belt. First, Dan praised him for his dedication, and Cane remembered his parting words: "Use your skill wisely."

He became very popular with his five dorm mates and became the unofficial leader of Block C. Rivalry among different sports and academics were routinely won by Block C, with Cane contributing a high percentage. He really came to the attention of the whole base when he was the only cadet to master the "hypothetical scenario" in a given battle. The punchline was that no men or minimum should be lost by the advancing team. Based on the data, most cadets came up with a lost factor of eight to fifteen from a hundred men. Cane simply wrote across his paper, "CANNOT BE DONE," which in fact was the right answer.

Up to this point in his life, Cane did not know what specifically what he wanted out of it. He remembered that he was very impressed with Sean Connery as 007, when he would introduce himself as...Bond...James Bond. It was a fantasy he had of himself as a young man, but he had matured enough to know that that was all it was a fantasy....

Britain granted Jamaica its Independence in August 1962. Although happy for his country, he realized that the Royal Fusiliers in Jamaica would be no more, and most likely, the men would be recalled to England. The romantic notion he had envisioned of been an elite soldier would no longer be viable. Based on communications, he was aware that Independent Jamaica would have its own army and would require men such as himself to take up leadership positions. His stay at Sandhurst after Independence was granted based on this premise. He could not, however, reconcile himself to the fact that he would be a big fish in a little pond. He would prefer to be a little fish in a big pond with the potential of getting bigger. He needed some time to think about his future, as the romantic idea of the army no longer held sway.

Cane graduated from Sandhurst in June 1967 with all the allocates they could bestow on him. He was first in every field except computer studies and counterintelligence, and that honor was shared with his fellow Jamaican Delroy Black. Each announcement was met with rapturous applause from his fellow cadets. Somehow, his dedication to everything he did also helped his block cadets, who shared his dorm, as they, too, excelled in their respective field. Delroy told Cane that he would be on the first flight home after his "extended" stay. He knew that Cane was undecided and wished him the best and hoped they would eventually meet up in Jamaica. At the end of term "disbanding party," although there was a pang of regret to see his close and fellow cadets probably for the last time, he felt elated that he had come through what he had chosen to do. With no consequence, as this was their last night, Cane snuck out when he got the chance and hopped a ride to Camberley.

Although no commitment was made, he thought he owed a young lady, whom he had an intimate relationship, the reason why she would not be seeing him again. Jennifer Keller was white, and their encounters were clandestine. She was young, vivacious, totally uninhibited, and could hold her own in any beauty pageant. An open relationship would have led to consequences for her in a small town where everyone knew each other business.

She worked at the tea shop beside the dojo, and after practice, he would stop in for tea and scones before returning to Sandhurst. Over time, small talk became more intimate, and finally to consummation. At first, he was a novelty, a young black man, having tea and scones in a rural setting. Not that he was the only black man in Camberely, as Cane had noticed quite a few from time to time and even other ethnic minorities. Here again Cane wondered why Sensi Fairclough had set up his dojo in this place. He was the first European to attain the title of "seven dan" in Taekwando in Japan. On his return to England, he had opened a dojo in London and after some years relocated here. The student enrollment was nine, including Cane, with seven men and two women, was hardly a money-making venture; but to each his own, thought Cane.

From day one Cane was impressed with his humility and even more so when he executed the various katas they would be required to learn. When Cane joined the dojo, there were three students ahead of him in terms of belts; Sensi Fairclough divided his time among them with equal dedication. He was always stressing that leaning this art was a way of maintaining mental superiority over physical aggression, and one should only resort to physical aggression if all avenues were closed. And even then he stressed with the minimal of force to diffuse the situation.

Based on prearranged signals beforehand, Jennifer was waiting for him at the dock house by the pond. She had snuck out of her parents' home to be with him. She knew it was her last night with him as she had heard about the graduation from others who knew the Sandhurst routine. On seeing him entering the boathouse, she rushed to him; her lips engulfed him, and she pulled hungrily for his tongue. As their passion heightened, they slipped to the floor and put out the fire that threatened to devour their souls. Once their breathing became normal and the afterglow of lovemaking enveloped them, Cane told her about his impending departure from Sandhurst. He was a bit taken aback when she said she knew, and he wondered if the intensity of her love-making had anything to do with that knowledge. They talked about life as black and white in England and even Jamaica and in the end decided that parting with good memories was the best way out. Cane remembered a similar parting in Jamaica with Opal, but there was no comparison. With Opal, he was not really concern about leaving her. With Jennifer, he felt a strange emptiness overwhelm him at the thought of their parting. Again, they embraced, holding each other tightly and without saying a word. After what seemed like an eternity in closeness, Cane felt her body relax as she positioned herself to look at him directly. Her gaze was penetrating, with her lips quivering as if she wanted to say something. After a few seconds she did.

"Cane," she began, "I did not fall in love with you quickly. I began to love you deeply overtime. Each time we met, natural or prearranged, I felt closer to you. As time passed and we became more intimate, I began to hope that you were feeling the same way about me and we had a future. I had gone to the library several times and looked up on Jamaica, as I felt that you would take me with you when you time was up here. I saw where politicians on both side of the political spectrum who had come to England to study returned with white wives and they were able to contribute meaningfully to the society. Even if it was not immediate, I figured I would complete my nursing and so would be able to be a part of whatever you were going to be in Jamaica. I was in love with a man; the fact that his skin color was different from mine was irrelevant to me, as I also knew that culturally we were not that far apart. That first time we had sex and you used a condom resulting in allergic rashes, I felt that was the end of our relationship. You even said after that when I promised to take necessary precaution how much our love-making had gone ballistic. Yes, Cane, I had lost any inhibitions. I had and gave myself wholly to you. Although you never said I love you, your actions spoke volumes, and I was prepared to wait until whatever was holding you back you would say those words to me. You are my first love, and if someone had told me as a child that I would end up loving a black man, I would think them crazy. I did have a black girlfriend named Hazel, and her older brother Dereck was always there for me." She paused, looked directly into Cane's face, and as he held her gaze, she was up and gone in a flash.

Cane sat there for a while, remembering the first time he had asked her for a date after many little conversations as he supped tea. He had invited her to see a play called *The Mousetrap* by Agatha Christie at the playhouse in London. She had looked at him, repeating the words…"a play" several times before saying okay. She told him she had an elder married sister that lived in the upscale suburbs of London called Hampstead and she would arrange for them to stay there overnight before returning the Sandhurst the next day as it might be tricky getting the last bus after the play. He was not sure about that arrangement, and she saw the perplexing look on his face. "Don't worry," she said. "My sister's husband is Maltese," and she was certain he would be welcomed. Her name was Pauline, and her husband was Shaok, with Tristan as their last names.

The following weekend he had gotten his weekend pass, and they met at the Charing Cross underground station early Saturday evening. The play started at eight p.m., so they spent the time taking in various notable sites in the area. From time to time, as they walked, she would hold his hands every now and then. Each time she touched, Cane he felt a slight shiver and wondered why. He had seen quite a number of "mix" couples in this the theater district of London. As they stood under Nelson column in Trafalgar Square, she told him that he was the first man to ever invite her to a play on their first date, all others she said was to a movie or to some pub for a drink. They both laughed.

During the play she held him and rested her head on his shoulders. He responded by holding close but gentle. She was right about getting transport back to Camberley as the last bus had left the area some thirty minutes ago. They took a cab up to her sister's place, and Cane was amused as the cab driver kept looking back at them with what could only be described as a scowl on his face. His demeanor did not change much when he pulled up before the address and was tipped handsomely.

Any misgivings Cane had about meeting Jennifer's sister were soon dispelled, as their greeting was warm and uninhibited. From the eyes and firm embrace, Cane knew that their welcome was genuine. They had tea and biscuits, and Sharock wanted to know all about Jamaica, as he said there was so much in common with Malta. In London, he was the head of a shipping company and jokingly said Cane could check him at a later date if he ever wanted to be in that business. They had no children, and it was a huge upstairs/downstairs four-bedroom townhouse; like almost every one of this side of the street. Based on the room he was shown, it was apparent that Sharock used it as an office as well. Jennifer was shown another further down the hall.

Just as he was dozing off, he heard the soft whoosh as the door was opened gently and the person was under the covers beside him before he was fully cognizant of what was taking place. He responded, however, fully as his mouth was searched for and his tongue pulled in a wild kissing frenzy. Jennifer was a top of him not making any noise, just devouring him, and she reached for his manhood, which had become incredible hard; she fitted him with a condom and inserted his manhood into her warm and wet womanhood. As they made love, the consequence of this action did not come into focus. He wondered of this action was meant to convey something about the direction the relationship was going. Later, as they lay nestled in each other arms, Cane felt a warm stream running down the side of his neck and knew that it was tears. She was crying softly. Before he could utter a word, she was up and left like a specter. That weekend became the forerunner of many more, and although on each occasion they entered separate bedrooms, it was obvious that Pauline and Sharock knew they were intimate whenever they stayed there.

The memories were pleasant, except for one incident that highlighted the disparity between young lovers of mix races and a homogeneous couple. Pauline and Sharock had gone away for that particular weekend. There were some good shows on the TV, and as they settled down Cane felt for a beer, only to discover there were not any in the fridge. He had noticed a liquor store down on the main street and decided to go and get some. Cane wandered why Jennifer was not too keen for him to go, but in the end, she relented. It was just late evening, and as he approached one entrance door, another opened, and about six young men spilled out on the sidewalk. Time froze as they took in Cane presence.

"Gor blimey," one finally said. "It's a darkie. What you doing up here, darkie?"

Before he could answer, another chimed in with, "Let's sort him out." Cane took that last statement to mean they were going to fight him. Cane did not like the odds, six against one. By now they had responded to the "let's sort him out" rallying cry and encircled him. Cane took up his karate stanza pose and said quite slowly but enunciating each word... "Which one of you is volunteering to die with me here and now?" They were all in a crouching position, moving in a circle around him. They stopped, and Cane could see the a look of puzzlement on their faces. "It is obvious," Cane continued, "that I can't fight all of you, but what I intend to do is to grab one of you." As he said that he made a grabbing motion, and they all jumped back. "And I don't care what the rest of you do. I will be holding that person in a death grip as I go down." Cane knew that it was a bluff, but the look on their faces told him they were not sure, and apparently, none of them were willing to die for a darkie.

The "Gor blimey" person's hand moved quickly as he whipped out a switchblade knife. Cane knew he was the first one he had to take out before the pummeling began. He was just about to take the initative, when he heard the *clang clang* of a police car (British police used bells on their cars instead of sirens). The group scattered as two police men alighted from the car. Cane was still in his karate pose.

The first to reach him, grabbed him, and forced up against the liquor store wall while asking, "What are you doing up here?" while the other began to pat him down, very heavy handed. By this time, a number of onlookers had gathered, and the policemen told them to disperse. Cane told them where he resided and what he was doing. He was bustled into the police car, after giving the driver the address. Thankfully, thought Cane, they did not turn on their siren bells or flash blue lights as they reached the address. Cane was told to remain in the car as one officer went and rang the bell to the townhouse. Even at the distance between house and car, Cane could see the look of a frightened Jennifer as she opened the door to a policeman. She kept looking past him to the car as she answered the questions he was asking. She even went back inside and brought out something to show him. Satisfied, after a few minutes, he returned to car said something to the driver and told Cane he could go. As Cane exited the car, he did not hear everything that the returning policemen said to the driver, but he did catch the word *Maltese*. Love making that night was very subdue, with Jennifer saying from time to time that she was sorry for what had happened. Yes, apart from that the memories were extremely pleasant.

Cane arrived back at Sandhurst just before first bugle and was glad that the strictness of the last few days before graduation was relaxed. He had encounter other cadets returning to base in the early morning, who apparently had "goodbyes" to say.

As he put his last item in his duffle bag, Batlavala appeared in the doorway with a huge grin. Cane has always liked him and enjoyed the way he spoke English. Many times, Cane would goad him into long conversation, just to enjoy the rhythm of his English and his hand movements as he spoke. "I have a little surprise for you," he said, handing Cane an envelope. Cane took it and opened it quickly. He was really surprised to see five twenty-pound bills flutter out. "What is this for?" Cane stammered.

"Oh, it is an accumulation of little bets I have made over time with other cadets that you would win this or that. This is your equal share." Cane just stood there, not knowing what to say, till finally they embraced and said their goodbyes.

He decided that he would stay in England, more than likely London, until he was sure of the direction he wanted to go. Although obligated to fulfill his commitment to his country, he requested and obtained permission from the Jamaican government to put his return to the island on indefinite hold. As he journeyed to London, his thoughts were filled with Jennifer and what if they had decided she should come to London with him. For the past few years, he had led a sheltered life from the general populous and wanted to have a feel of what the reception to a black man was like in the greater community. Then and only then he would decide his move.

It was a glorious, warm, and sunny mid-June day when he arrived in London. He headed straight for the youth hostel address he was given at Sandhurst. He was told that they probably would not have any accommodation for him, but they were in the business of helping students from all over the world find lodgings. The hostel foyer was full of a variety of nationalities and a gaggle of languages abound. Working his way to the front, he saw a sign which read, "Seeking Accommodation" and joined that line. He was surprised how quickly it moved, and on reaching the desk, the harried-looking young man said, "English?"

Cane nodded and was a handed a paper. The paper contained a list of twenty student housing, and some were with phone numbers. The paper also instructed those with luggage where to put and it and must be retrieved within twenty-four hours. Armed with a London map, Cane plotted his route to take in those that had no phone numbers. Based on the crowd at the hostel, he figured that the phone number ones would be the first to be checked out. They were all clustered within a one-mile radius of the hostel, so he figured he would spend the rest of the day seeking accommodation. The first house was about twenty minutes away, and on opening the gate he heard a woman's voice from the basement saying, "If you are coming about accommodation, it's gone." He ticked off that one and moved to the next. All the houses were similar in this area. Three to four stories high, with a basement. Again, he opened a gate, which creaked, and walked up the very short walk to the front door. He saw the curtains at the ground floor window moved as it fell back, and since he did not hear any discouraging sound, he rang the bell and stepped back. Nothing happened. He was certain someone was home because the curtains moved, so he rang again.

After the third attempt, he became convinced that for whatever reason his presence was not welcomed. After several more attempts in which he was told by the person who opened the door that they do not rent to "darkies," he felt very despondent. He was feeling hungry as well and stopped into the English equivalent of McDonald's to have a bite. For a moment, he wondered if he would be told we don't serve "darkies," but seeing others like himself scattered around, he felt a bit more composed. Most tables and booths had space to accommodate more than one person, so after receiving his burger, drink, and fries, he sat in a booth with only one person opposite. As he slurped, the reality of the situation came down on him like an elephant squashing a mouse into the ground.. He was a black man seeking accommodation in a prejudice society. Landlords and landladies who gave their names to the youth hostel had to sign that they would not discriminate against the students who came seeking accommodation. But reality and practicality were too different things. Even if students who were discriminated against complained to the youth hostel, there was very little they could do as the demand for accommodation was greater than the supply. He must have sighed audibly because the man sitting opposite to him said, "Are you all right? Cane looked into the steady gaze of a clean-shaven young white man of about thirty who had finished his meal and was leisurely reading the *London Times*. His tan was not local, and his facial expression as he made his inquiry was genuine. Before Cane could answer, he continued, "My name is Jason Higgins. I am a journalist for this newspaper," pointing to the Times, "and your sigh was so pronounced I just wondered—"

Cane cut him off. "I am sorry, I did not mean to disrupt your meal."

As he apologized, Jason had dipped into his waistcoat pocket and produced a card, which he handed to Cane. It confirmed Jason's identity, and to this day Cane wondered why he poured out his frustrations to a total stranger. On reflection, he knew it was the rejection he faced as a man, an intelligent black man. Jason listened without interruption. As a journalist, he was taken with the story this young man had told and wondered if there was worth enlarging into something else. He decided that what was taking place was common, and he was sure his editor would not wish him to pursue this any farther unless it happened to someone really important. Jason reached into his waistcoat pocket once more, retrieved a card, and wrote something on the back of it. As he handed it to Cane, he arose, shook, Cane's hand, and made his exit. Cane stood for a while before reading what was on the card. It was an address, according to his map about ten minutes away, in Earls Court where he might find "something." It was an office in a house, and on entering, he came upon a middle-aged white man, not locally tanned, shuffling some papers on his desk. His "come in" and "what can I do for you" were genuine enough. Cane introduced himself and handed him the card Jason had given him. He smiled, invited Cane to sit down, and introduced himself. His name was Gary Waverley, married, with two teenage boys and an adult girl; he owned a few buildings around the area; his secretary was off sick; and he vacationed a lot in Barbados and Jamaica. Cane could not help but smile with his last remark. Yes…he had one or two bedsitters available at the moment. He pulled a paper from his desk, pointing out that it was a month-to-month lease and what would be required. The bedsitter he had in mind for Cane would be at one of his buildings on the Earls Court Road. Cane met all his requirements and was handed a key and a receipt for the money he had deposited on this unseen bedsitter.

If the tidiness of the office and the man's demeanor were anything to go by, he figured the bedsitter would be clean. As he arose and was halfway through the door, he felt he had to ask the question that was bothering him. As he turned, he met Gary's eyes, twinkling, and a broad smile on his face.

"I was wondering when you were going to ask…why?" he said. He turned a photo frame on his desk towards Cane. Cane smiled and left to go back to the hostel to pick up his duffle bag. He was in high spirits now. A chance meeting with a stranger in a café had changed his whole outlook. Not that he would not encounter prejudice in the future, he did not kid himself, but a white man who had married a black woman and had three gorgeous children was a rarity in England.

Much later on, Cane found out that towards the end of the war, his landlord was injured, and it was his wife, then a black nurse, helping on the RAF base, that literally nursed him back to health. They fell in love and got married. Bombed-out houses were cheap in London then, and they decided to invest their savings into real estate as London rebuilt. As the years went by, they invested more and more, and when it became apparent that Caribbean immigrants were flooding into England and housing was acute, their investments paid off handsomely. Another class of immigrants were also flooding into England—students. Based on her own experiences of prejudice, Gary's wife persuaded him to consolidate all their holdings into specific and manageable units and cater for students only. Most of the students coming to England were government sponsored, and the various Caribbean High Commissions would seek accommodation for them. This was done, and Cane was thankful to Mrs. Waverley for her foresight.

The bedsitter was just off the Earls Court Road. The house had four stories and a basement, with each floor divided into single-room flats and bedsitters. While flats had a bedroom, living room, kitchenette, and small bathroom, bedsitters had a single bed, closet, chair, table, washbasin, and a little alcove with a single electric burner. The bathroom was at the end of each floor hallway. Settling in, he became aware of the other Caribbean nationals who lived there as he would hear different accents coming from above and sometimes below. He had yet to meet anyone specific with whom he could exchange banter. Doors open, doors close, a shadow here, a shadow there. Cane realized that you could live in a crowded house and yet never meet anyone, as there was no focal point for social gathering.

Returning from one of his familiarization walks a couple days later, he met a young lady at the front steps just about to enter. On seeing her, he was overwhelmed by her natural beauty. She wore a tight-fitting body blouse and a Calvin Klein slacks. To say she was extremely attractive would be an understatement. With close cropped hair in the style of "curly Afro," a complexion of coffee just barely diluted with a touch of milk, and a smile which revealed glistening white, even incisors made Cane strangle in an effort to say "wow" and hello at the same time. So, nothing came out but a gulp. A sign which read, "Dangerous Curves" could easily be hung around her neck. She was about five feet, nine inches tall and was really a vision of loveliness. The smile she gave him as their eyes met was one of long-time old friends. He had never seen her before, and he quickly completed the opening of the front door as she struggled with a couple of shopping bags. He took two from her and held the door open. As she passed by, he could not help but take in the slight aroma of an expensive perfume.

It turned out she had the flat adjacent to his bedsitter on the third floor. As they walked up the stairs, introductions were made, and nationality given. She was a second-year student nurse at the Hammersmith Hospital, came from Barbados, and her name was Mercedes Braithwaite. What usually took a couple of leaps and bounds to his door now took forever, as they literally stopped on each step, chatting as they made their way up. As they reached her door and she positioned her key, Cane did not want to openly intrude on her privacy, but secretly, he did. She was extremely attractive, and after four years at Sandhurst without laying eyes on an attractive black female, she was more than icing on a cake. On reflection, he wondered at that point in time how quickly Jennifer was out of focus. He was hoping against hope that she would invite him in to her flat, and most of all, he hoped that she was not already going steady or had a boyfriend. He sighted internally; that would be too much to wish for from one so attractive. He wondered if his "yes" acceptance came out too quickly when she asked him if he would like to join her for dinner, which she was about to prepare. She smiled as she turned her key, and her door opened into a gorgeously furnished flat. He was awestruck, and it showed.

"My father is not too bad off and supports me." She smiled as in answer to the question he never asked but was written on his face As she finished unpacking the groceries, Cane told her about himself, even to the point that he did not know what to do with himself at this present moment. They talked a lot as she busied herself cooking, and he would fetch and carry little items for the pot as the cooking demanded it. He learned that this was her second year of a three-year nurses' course at the hospital, and as such, she could live off campus. During her first year, all students virtually lived under curfew at the hospital hostel. She was lucky to find this flat, as the hostel life was becoming stifling and she could not wait to be on her own. At nineteen, this was the first time she was on her own, and only since January of this year. Cane wondered if he dared to ask about her "other half" but decided not to as he was sure this would not be their last meeting and events in the future would answer that question. That did not stop him from interjecting from time to time the fact that he was free, single, and disengaged. After about the third interjection, he realized that there was no reciprocal mention of her personal associations, so he decided to stay away from that topic. The dinner was a typical Barbadian dish of cuckoo and flying fish, she explained. Cane had never had it before, but he took serving after serving with relish.

As they ate, Mercedes would from time to time look keenly at this stranger that she had invited for dinner. Why did she do it? she kept asking herself. He was a Jamaican, and as far as she was concerned Jamaican men must be carefully dealt with at arm's length. They had a reputation of loving and leaving, according to her friends and family. Well, she knew he was a Jamaican by his accent, but there was just something about him that said…"Please invite me in for dinner." Inside, he talked a lot without bragging and came across as a young man who was waiting to embrace life head on and take care of whatever obstacle it placed in his way. The last few months had not given her many opportunities to socialize. It was study, exams, study, exams.

These last few months when she was on her own, she frequented the West Indian Students Center and had many acquaintances of both gender, but no one male in particular.

Jamaican males dominated there, and every now and then when she felt particularly lonely she would accept a date to a movie or a cricket match in which the WISC was involved. Her dates ended at her door, and a "good night peck on the cheek" was her best offering. On two occasions her dates had moved their faces quickly to receive a full mouth-to-mouth, but she had avoided them and made sure she crossed those persons off for future dates. Subsequent requests were met with…"I have to study…" and in time she became a part of a crowd without affinity to any one in particular. This young man whom she had invited to dinner was somehow different. He spoke confidently and had a very disarming smile. She found herself listening to him as he espouse, although briefly, on different subjects. From when they met at the door to entering her flat, she had learned a great deal about him. Perhaps his lack of complimenting her on how gorgeous she was etc. made her tolerated his presence more. She knew that she was not God's gift to men, but pretty close. From when she was a child, she graduated from "what a pretty little girl," "what a lovely young lady," to "what a gorgeous young woman"; other superlatives were thrown in from time to time. She often wondered if men saw her as a sex object first or a woman. This young man gave no hint of his thinking. She smiled as she remembered the two occasions when he would interject "as a single man" into some point of view as he sees it.

After the meal, Cane helped her to do the dishes and was told that she had a couple of girlfriends whom like herself had branched out on their own. For a while they had planned to rent a three-bedroom together, but at the last moment she realized that she wanted her own space, hence here she was.

"I am going to the West Indian Students Center tomorrow evening. Would you like to come?" she said out of the blue.

Again, his "yes" was quick. He did not know what the WISC was, but if it was hell, and she was going, he would be right there.

"Okay, I get in about six-thirty p.m. It's not far, so we can have dinner there. Right now, it's time for my beauty sleep," she said, smiling. "So off you go." Cane thanked her for a wonderful evening and exited her flat to his dull and drab bedsitter, so it seemed in contrast. Initially, as he went to the open door that she stood beside, he wanted to try and embrace her. At the last second, he dispelled that notion, nodded, smiled, and left.

He fell asleep almost instantly with the picture of her smile in his mind and the beautiful Barbadian English accent that came from her when she spoke. As Mercedes closed the door, she could not help smiling to herself; she saw for a brief second the look in his eyes as he came towards her and wondered if he had tried to embrace her what she would have done.

Cane could not wait for six-thirty p.m. to come to next day. He spent the day lazing around and looking at the clock. The last time he looked it was four p.m., and when he heard the rap on his door, he was aroused from a deep sleep. He sprang from the bed and jerked the door open, just as Mercedes was turning away. Hearing the door opened, she turned around. "Oh, I thought you had forgotten that we had a date or had someone with you," she said seriously.

"I must have dozed off, sorry," Cane replied lamely. *Oh God*, he thought, *my first date and I was about to mess it up*. "I am ready, let me get my shoes." Cane was looking forward to this moment for the whole day, and when it happened, he was asleep. He wondered why she had put in the "someone with you" bit. She had on Calvin Klein jeans that highlighted her lower curves and a body blouse which did the same for her upper form.

As they walked down Earls Court Road, she informed him about the WISC. It was a multifaceted building, housing a library, games room, showers, lounge, ballroom, meeting room, TV room, canteen, and bar. Students from all over the Caribbean gathered there on a daily basis. Not only for the comradeship but to basically chill out from the daily grind of working and studying and living in hell holes. Some bedsitters had no heat, so in the winter students would hang out until the WISC closed at eleven-thirty p.m., then make a dash for their last train or bus to reach home. They finally reached an imposing building in Collingham Gardens, and they entered. The foyer was huge, and while she was signing him in as her guest, several other guys would embrace her in welcoming hellos. It was dinner time, and she bought two tickets from the person whom he later learned was the assistant warden. She said that there was steak and pork chops on the menu, along with rice and peas and mixed vegetables. Following her example in obtaining the meals, they sat down at a table for two. Continuously throughout the meal, guys would come up to greet her, and she would introduce Cane as a "friend." After the meal was over, she took Cane on a grand tour of the building, with men and women making all sorts of flippant remarks as they poked their heads into each room. She was very popular, Cane thought.

Just before eleven p.m., as they made their way down the main stairs to go into the foyer, Cane was introduced to the warden who ran the center… Mr. Ivanhoe Bryant. He, too, was from Barbados. Cane had recognized quite a number of accents, and predominantly Jamaican as he toured the Center. He noticed also that although ostensibly for Caribbean tudents, quite a number of Commonwealth students were there from African countries. As they walked back to their building, she told him that to become a member of the WISC, all he had to do was become a full- or part-time student. She would sign his recommendation, and he could hang out there. The idea appealed to Cane because there were some evenings in the past when he was tired of fish and chips and all the other "English fast foods." The WISC would provide him with a meal he would enjoy, and at virtually the same price or even cheaper, plus the added advantage of meeting other students.

"How did you become so popular there?" he asked. Before she could answer, he continued, "How did you find out about the WISC?" He did not want her to think that he was prying with the first question.

"Oh," she said, "the British Council informs all students about it on their arrival in England to study. My girlfriends and I use to go down there every Saturday night that we were off as first-year student nurses. With four of us, we were popular. The guys there would book dates with us even before we knew if we were going to be off the next Saturday. The only thing was that we had to be back in the hostel by twelve a.m., and sometimes the guys wanted us to go to parties after the Center closed. We never did, because if management did a bed count that night and found anyone missing, that person would be thrown off the course and out."

A picture began to form in Cane's mind. She was basically available for the last year; yes, it was possible that she had not formed any meaningful relationship with anyone here, but there could still be someone waiting in Barbados. They reached their building.

On their way up the stairs, Cane wondered what he should do as they parted. Should he make a definitive move? As he approached his door, Mercedes relieved him of his quandary by quickly kissing him on his cheek with a "see ya," and before he could say a word, she had glided into her flat.

Cane entered his room and began to undress slowly. The night was hot, and his little fan did very little to cool him. Mercedes had left him hot. "See ya," not "see you tomorrow," just "see ya." Was he taking too much for granted? Was her warming personality made him just "a friend," as he was introduced, or could there be more? After all, it was only their second time spent together.

Over the next week or so, Cane did not see Mercedes. Whenever he knocked at her door, she was either out or indicated through the door that she would call him later. She never did. *What did I do or did not do?* Cane kept wondering. Did she have a guy? Was he there when he knocked? He tried to forget her and busied himself in sorting out other aspects of his life. He needed a part-time job, as his stipend would soon run out. A job which gave him the flexibility to attend classes and enough to live on. As a former Commonwealth student holding a British passport, he was entitled to go to any university that would accept him without tuition cost to himself. The "A" levels he obtained at Sandhurst would be his matriculation requirement. He signed on at the Holborn Collage of Law to begin a law course in October. His student form to join the WISC was signed by Mercedes and pushed under his door, just as he had done initially for her to sign. He now frequented the WISC, and within days found his niche in the political arm of the WISC known as the West

Indian Student Union. He became a vocal member. Political dialogue was held every day in the meeting room and sometimes continued from when the Center opened at eleven a.m. to its closure at eleven-thirty p.m. Kendrick Saul was the president of the Union, and in a very short while they became close friends. He was also a Jamaican and a second-year law student. Cane discovered that about ninety percent of all the male students at the WISC were budding lawyers, and the same percentage in nursing for the females.

The Vietnam War was heating up, and every day more and more students became vocal about it. As a military student, Cane felt that America should not be in Vietnam. He expressed this opinion very strongly at WISU forum every day. Kendrick encouraged him and asked him to participate on panels that discussed the American gathering involvement in Vietnam. By early July, more students were on holiday and frequented the Center. Cane found that he was the main person that students sought information from or was asked to clarify points on the Vietnam War. Kendrick suggested that they should go one step further and vocalize their ideas at a more public forum. It was decided that the following Sunday he would expound on his ideas at Hyde Park Speakers Corner.

This Speakers Corner was legendary in English folklore. Anyone could speak their mind here without fear of prosecution. There were two provisos: one, you could not slander; and two, you could not use expletive. He would never forget that Sunday evening. He was about five minutes in denouncing the American involvement in Vietnam, when he realized that a sizeable crowd had gathered. The crowd grew as the evening wore on, and by nightfall, he had several hundred listeners. Someone had handed him a megaphone, and this enhanced his tirade even further. The long summer evenings, getting dark at about nine p.m., gave him amply opportunities to really blast America's involvement in Vietnam. As it got darker and the crowd began to disperse, the megaphone giver introduced himself as Tyrone Blake. He said he was the president of the London chapter of "Rally for Peace." It was a non-aligned peace movement, and he inquired about Cane. He said that he has been here at Speakers Corner for about four Sundays, vocalizing about the American involvement in Vietnam; the most crowds he ever generated was about forty persons. What he saw blew his mind at Cane's oratory mastery. He invited Cane to come to meet other presidents of the different chapters. It would be on a Wednesday at two p.m., and he would call to give me the exact date. Cane accepted the invitation.

As he made his way home, Cane reflected about just what took place. Speakers Corner was so called because anyone could go there, safe in the knowledge that they had immunity for what they said as long as it was not slanderous or expletives were used. But one could make insinuations, and this they did in abundance. He smiled to himself at times as he remembered how as his confidence grew, his oratory became more commanding and forceful. Quite a lot of what he said was factual, while he interjected philosophical and moral arguments at the precise time in his speech. At Sandhurst, he had read quite a lot of military journals about the French involvement in Indo-China, and their subsequent withdrawal was one of his favorite topics of interest. So lost in his thoughts of the last few hours that he looked up and realized that he had reached home. Reaching the top of the stairs, he wondered if he should knock on Mercedes door, but decided against it. He was feeling good, and a no answer or "call you later" would only deflate the feeling he had.

The next morning, as Cane reached his door to let himself out, he saw that a note was pushed under it. It was just yesterday he had removed a tape he used to seal the gap between door and floor, as he had seen what looked like an insect scurry away when he entered some few nights ago. Mercedes was not paying him any attention, so sealing the gap would be of no account. It could be a cockroach or whatever. Anyhow, he had decided to seal the door. His heart accelerated, and he opened the note with trembling hands. Instinctively, he knew that it was from Mercedes and wondered if its contents spelled gloom or gladness. It was the latter. Mercedes wanted to see him when she got home. The note simply said, "Can I see you later?" He felt light-headed, and sipped several cups of coffee at the diner where he usually had breakfast. He timed his morning risings to coincide with reaching the WISC just as it opened. As he stepped inside, several other students were already there, and some of them broke out in applause. He was confused, and his confusion showed as he looked around, wondering what this adulation was all about. Kendrick ushered him into the meeting room, grabbed his hand, and began to pump it vigorously. "You were on TV last night," he gushed.

"What? How?" Cane was lost for words.

Kendrick said that apparently ITV was doing a vox-pop the same time Cane was speaking, and on seeing the largest crowd around him, the TV crew filmed him and was given two minutes of airtime on the late-night news. Again, Cane was lost for words. Before he could answer to the sizeable gathering that was now in the meeting room, he was interrupted by the intercom, which announced that there was a call for him on the public phone number one in the foyer. As he excused himself and headed towards the phone, another call came over the intercom that he was wanted also on phone number two.

He answered phone one. It was Tyrone Blake who congratulated him on his TV appearance and confirmed their two p.m. meeting on Wednesday.

"Sorry to keep you waiting, I was on the other phone," he began as he picked up phone two.

"Miss me," the voice began. His heart stopped; he felt the blood rushed to his head; it was Mercedes.

Before he could answer, she spoke, and he was glad she did because he did try to answer, but no words came out.

"Thomas"—she called him Thomas, not Cane—"I am sorry about the way I treated you lately, but since you did not have a phone at home I kept missing you to tell you what was happening." Before he could get a word in edgewise, she continued, "I had end-of-term exams, and my friends and I decided that we would group study after our shift ended at Megan's flat. By the time I got home, it was late, and I had early call for the last two weeks and most morning just rushed out. It is only because I just finished my final exam paper and I figured that you were at the WISC that I am able to call. Did you get my note?" Cane's heart had settled down and the constraints on his vocal cord gone.

"An earlier note would have sufficed," his voice had an accuser's tone as the thoughts about her for the last two weeks came rushing into his mind.

"I was not certain how to word it, and plus I did not want to leave a note by your door so that anybody passing could see this paper on the floor and read it. I had no tack or tape to paste it on. There was some kind of mat or something blocking under the door." She had a point. Cane's mind relaxed, and they talked about everything and nothing encompassing the last two weeks. In her voice, Cane realized that there were more than just friends talking, and he hoped she picked up the inflections in his. Finally, it was decided that there was movie, *Ben Hur*, that she wanted to see at the Odeon Cinema in Hammersmith. Could they meet outside at six-thirty p.m.? During his conversation with Mercedes, the intercom kept announcing that there were calls for him on the different phone lines. Cane ignored them. Only Mercedes was in his thoughts.

As he walked towards the meeting room, Cane remembered meeting Megan and her two other friends. The first time he and Mercedes had come to the WISC and he was introduced as "a friend." At one point he could not help classing them as the three musketeers and Mercedes. They were all attractive young women, Mercedes the jewel, focused on their primary objective to become nurses and knew how to achieve it.

Cane spent the rest of the day in the meeting room waiting for six-thirty p.m. to approach. In the meantime, the phone calls of a congratulatory nature kept pouring in from students, some of whom he did not even know by name.

As he reflected on the events that overtook him, he realized that yesterday no one knew him, today he was sort of a national figure, a voice for anti-American sentiments in England. He was a non-entity, not even the leader of any "movement." Now a telecast had propelled him into the spotlight. He was the face of the anti-war protesters in England.

It was easy to spot Mercedes in the small crowd in front of the cinema as he alighted from the bus. As she saw him, she rushed to him, and they embraced with a light kiss on each other's cheek. The movie was a long one, and Cane felt very comfortable as she nestled in his shoulders with his arm around her. She would hide her face into his chest from time to time as a scene became gory, and he would kiss her lightly on the cheek when she pulled apart as if to reassure that it was okay to resume looking.

During the famous chariot race, she dug her fingers deep into his forearm, and although it was painful, he said nothing. When she realized that her action was hurtful, she would apologize with a light kiss full on his lips. She seemed so happy. He guessed the weight of her exams was finished and this was her first chance of really relaxing. Cane wished there were more chariot races. They took a cab home, as the movie finished very late. Reaching to the top of the stair, Cane had no doubt by her body language she wanted him to stay with her. He was not wrong. As she closed the door behind them, he stood there and watched her. She came gliding into his arms, with her mouth searching for his. The kiss was long, sweet, and searching. It was at this point that he realized that the way he was kissing her was not indicative of just wanton passion. Of course he wanted her, but he also wanted to know that she wanted him as well. She finally broke their embrace, nibbled his ear, and very seductively said, "Be gentle," as she led him to the bedroom. There was a silence.

They did not immediately begin to strip off their clothes and rush into bed to satisfy the feelings that had enveloped them earlier. Instead, she broke the silence with, "Let's have some coffee and talk," as she seated him down. Cane welcomed the intervention. His emotions were very unstable at this moment, and he needed a little time to focus specifically on the step he was about to take and the possible ramifications. One thing he was sure about, in all his dealings with women, he had never felt the type of emotions he now felt with anyone before. On reflection, he now knew that Jennifer was raw sex, highlighted by the knowledge that he was black and she was white. It was his first encounter with another woman not of his race, and the knowledge that he was crossing a cultural barrier had excited him more than normal. Another place, another time, and he would be hung if just his thoughts about a white female was known. Mercedes curled up in the settee, sipping from a huge cup. His cup was smaller, and he sipped rapidly. There was still an awkward silence. If this was a game, he thought it was very emotional one for him. Then he realized that although the prospect of making love to her was making the hot coffee seem cold, he saw something more than a quick bang, wallop, thank you, madam. He felt that he wanted more than sex from her. But what…what is more? he thought.

"Thomas, or you prefer to be called Cane, are you sure that you want to have sex with me?" she said suddenly as she removed the mug from her lips.

"More than anything else," he replied in a steady and convincing tone, "and you can call me whatever name that suits you."

"I will call you TAC," she said

"TAC, how? Why?"

"Thomas Alexander Cane."

He smiled; the acronym of his name never dawned on him before, and he slipped over and kissed her lightly on the lips. "TAC it is," he said. Cane…Thomas Alexander (the James Bond fantasy took over).

"TAC, listen, when I was in high school, I had a boyfriend, my first love, really. He was a final-year student at the university, and I thought that we would be together once he got his degree. He never let me feel that at seventeen to his twenty-one, there would be any problem. I have always looked more mature than my years." She sighed, closed her eyes, and Cane could see a little pain clouding her face. He embraced her slightly.

"My life was really shattered when he left, after completing his degree without even a goodbye. One of his friends told me he had left on the morning flight for Trinidad. I had gone to see him at the campus hostel."

Again, she paused, and TAC held her a little closer.

"My parents kept silent throughout my moping around the house until they agreed that I should go to England and fulfill my wish of becoming a nurse." She was now resting her head on Cane's shoulder. "So here I am. When I saw you that first day, I don't know why I invited you to dinner. But after we met and I disappeared for two weeks, while I was doing exams, I found myself thinking about you a lot. My first thought, after my final paper, was to get in touch with you. TAC, I am not asking for any commitment or promise, just be honest with me in whatever we are doing." Cane turned her head found her mouth and kissed her long and passionately.

"I promise," he said, breaking, before kissing her once again.

Their lovemaking was passionate and subdued at the same time. Sometimes they would try to devour each other, while within a short time they would resort to the slow thrusts and give in to the rhythm of their bodies, only for the excitement to develop once more, rising to a crescendo of passion. This continued as Cane explored her Venus-like body, noting the breasts that quivered and rippled to settle into firmness as he ran his tongue over them, and the way the nipples shot up like exploding volcanos as he kissed them. Bra manufactures would sigh deeply if they saw the firmness of the two majestic orbs which did not require any support. Although, in his estimation, they stood out as a testament to the favor she was doing them by wearing one. When that glorious moment of rapture came, it erupted with such intensity that it left them both breathless and panting. Cane did not smoke, and neither did she, so they lay there, locked in each other arms as their passion waned.

"You know, if someone broke into this flat at this very moment, you would be on your own," Cane said.

It took a few seconds before she replied, "Why?"

"Because I am so weak that I would not be able to lift a finger to defend you," he said.

"You better hope that the person is not gay, or you would be in trouble, because I could not even be able to call the police." They both laughed. It was the laugh of two persons who had found a sexual compatibility that was rare. Cane let out a little giggle.

"What now?" she inquired

"Oh, I just remembered a situation where a couple was awakened by an intruder in their bedroom. The man was quickly tied up, and the intruder bent over the woman still lying in the bed. He then got up and went to the bathroom. The husband, fearing for their lives, said quickly, 'My love, I recognize that prison uniform the man has on. Obviously, he just escaped, and he fancies you, as I saw him begin to nibble at your ears. Do whatever he wants, and probably, he will spare us. The wife gave a little laugh. 'You are right,' she said. 'He just escaped from prison, but he was not nibbling at my ears. He was asking me where the Vaseline was, and I told him in the medicine chest in the bathroom. He has gone to fetch it. It is you he fancies, so you do your thing.'" They both laughed and drifted into blissful sleep in each other arms.

Cane awoke and glanced at the clock on the night table; it read four-twenty a.m.. He was still nestled into Mercedes' arms. He felt his manhood begin to stiffen, they were both still naked, and was just about to get up, when Mercedes groaned softly and pulled him even closer to her. In a second, she slid under him and guided his manhood inside her warm, pulsating womanhood. How do you improve on perfection? This time she held him tightly so that there was very little movement from him; she gyrated her lower body in a circular motion beneath him. At first she did it slowly, moving a little faster after each circular movement. He thought his mind and body were going to explode. And explode they did, in unison as if choreograph by an unseen master.

Cane remembered very little after that moment and awoke to the sweet smell of coffee brewing fresh. He could hear the splash of water and movement in the bathroom. The bedside clock showed nine-twenty a.m..

"Ah, you are awake, sleepyhead," Mercedes said, as she emerged from the bathroom wrapped in a towel robe. She came over to him and planted a good morning kiss on his cheek. The fresh scent of her washed body and the cologne she had on was enough to affect him. She pulled the sheet off him, and when she saw that his manhood was on the rise again, she laughed. "Save it for later, Romeo," she said as she rushed back into the bathroom to complete her morning libation. He was surprised that she had that effect on him and knew that if he had shown a positive attitude, they would more than likely have make love again. But she was right, there would be many, many more later.

They had a leisurely breakfast of eggs, bacon, and toast, washed down with several mugs of fresh coffee. Cane had showered and felt full of energy with a glowing feeling inside. He looked across the table, and there sat a woman that he felt sure he could spend his life with. Young, brainy, beautiful, and a wonderful sex mate. They ate in silence, only asking to pass this or that as required. There was so much he wanted to say about last night and what it meant to him. Why was he so afraid to talk with one woman who had just let him feel like a man in a million, yet he could mesmerize hundreds even thousand at Speakers Corner?

"Are you going to WISC today?" she inquired
"Yes, I should be there as usual all day"
"Okay. I have to meet my friends later this morning and do some shopping, and they will be having dinner here. You can join us if you want." Cane wanted and agreed that he should be back by seven p.m. Cane asked her if she had heard anything about his TV debut. She said no and enthusiastically asked Cane to fill her in on what it was all about. He backtracked to the point where Kendrick had encouraged him to go public as to how West Indian students felt about America's involvement in Vietnam and the whole Speakers Corner episode with the Peace Movement President, culminating in the TV

broadcast. Before he got out the last word, she was around the table, hugging and giving him kisses all over his face. He was surprised at her reaction because, as a nurse, he did not think that she would be politically polarized about issues like the Vietnam War.

After they finished breakfast and began clearing up the dishes, Cane could see that she was deep in thought. "TAC, sit down and don't interrupt until I am finished," she said as she put away the last plate on the dish drainer. "I don't want you to think that I am rushing anything, but this is how I see things. You are living across the hall from me, we are lovers, I don't mind if you move in with me and we share the flat. You can contribute whatever you want because I know how some men feel if they think they are supported by a woman; no female friends here when I am out, and I will have no male friends here. All I ask is that you be honest with me in everything." She was looking directly into his eyes and his face as she spoke, and they did not waiver as she waited for his answer. When she had started, Cane thought because of what took place last night she was going to ask for a strong commitment from him. God, if she had asked him to marry her, the way he felt, he would have said yes. Instead, he rose, slowly took her into his arms, and kissed her passionately but tenderly.

"Does that answer your questions?" he asked as he broke the kiss.

"Oh yes, oh yes," she breathed.

Although the apartment was a swell one, it was revamped to accommodate one person with a little elbow room. In the time Cane had spent there, he realized that they would need a larger apartment to be comfortable for two. He made the suggestion about moving and was further taken aback when she agreed wholeheartedly. They would begin looking for a larger and even nicer apartment as funds would permit. He called Mr. Waverley and was delighted when he was told that a larger one bedroom would be available at the end of the month. Cane knew that Mercedes received a generous stipend from her family, although he never asked how much. He was on a stipend from the British Council, which would end at the end of September as he was no longer a British subject. Granted, ninety-nine percent of all apartments (flats) were furnished, and one could move in right away, but to get that feeling of your own home, you needed to add your personal little bric-a-brac. The flat available was at a building called Hazlettt House, a three-story building with a basement, which consisted of a variety of flats from extra-large one-bedrooms to two-bedroom units. The extra-large one suited fine. Plus, they had the extra luxury of a private phone. Mercedes spent the next few days fixing up the flat. She would ask his advice here and there as has not for him to feel completely left out, but most of the ideas of interior decorating were hers. The transformation was complete within a week, and anyone who saw it before they moved in and saw it now would have sworn that it was a different flat from the original. They had a candlelight dinner on the first Saturday night and finished with crazy lovemaking on the plush carpet. Both were awakened from their spent passion at about the same time and climbed into bed, and without saying anything, reached for each other immediately. This time the lovemaking was more sedate. Crazy on the carpet, because they changed positions often, chased each around the flat, and had pillow fights.

Monday at the WISC, there was some great news for Cane. A job as relief barman was open, and it was his for the taking. The hours would be from six to eleven p.m. every day and every other weekend off. The pay was also adequate enough for him to make a meaningful contribution to his household obligations.

He called Mercedes, and she wanted him to return to celebrate his good fortune. As they talked, he could hear the tease in her voice as she dared him to return. He finally won out with a "Later I will make it up." That night, she held him to his promise.

Tyrone Blake called and wanted to know if he was available for two p.m. on Wednesday. He did not have to work until six, so he agreed to meet as schedule. The next day ran off quickly, and here he was at Hyde Park Corner, meeting with Ashley Boone from Liverpool, Gillian Prendegast from Manchester, and John Rainford from Leeds. They were presidents of the Peace Movement from their respective universities. Adulation and congratulations were in their greetings, and they just could not get over how he was able to attract so many people so quickly. Ashley noted that what impressed her was that the gathering she had seen on TV was a mixture of a great cross-section of people of different ages.

This meeting was basically twofold, they asserted. One was to meet him in person and assess him as an individual. Once they reached a consensus, the second option was to plan a strategy for upcoming demonstrations. As they talked, John was recording the meeting. He explained that the meeting would be typed up later for their files. Private firms made donations from time to time, so they tried to keep accurate records of everything they did. After about an hour or so, it was agreed that there would be a mass meeting here on two Sundays from now, and Cane would be the main speaker. Based on enquirers they and other groups were receiving, they were sure the meeting would be indeed a massive one. The topics on which he would speak on were agreed. Afterwards, a protest march on the US Embassy in Grosvenor Square would take place.

Mercedes was working her day shift, leaving home about five a.m. to be at work by six. She got off at two p.m. and would come to the Center to use the library, have dinner with Cane, and both would walk home. It became very obvious to other WISC regulars that these two had indeed become a twosome. Sometimes, she would call to say that she is doing a special dinner and would have it warm for him when he reached home.

Thomas always introduced himself as Thomas Cane, but without exception everyone one called him by his surname—Cane. Mercedes reminded him that he always said Cane first, then...Thomas (he still had that 007 introduction in his mind). The WISC job as relief barman was ideal. He now had funds to more than contribute to the household. It was never said between himself and Mercedes, but during pillow talk she would use phrases like, "At home I am going to do this or do that." Never going into any details, but Cane understood from those snippets of information that as soon as her nursing course was over, she was heading back to Barbados. He was about to study law in October, which in itself would take three more years. He had no doubt that he loved this woman. Vibrant, beautiful, brainy, and matched his expectations in everything. He had no doubts also that he matched hers. So, what was the problem? he asked of himself. Would she be willing to wait until he qualified as a lawyer, or would her desire to return to Barbados take precedence over her love for him? Was the time frame of their relationship too short for long-term commitments to be made? There were so many little things he had taken for granted without exploring the outcome. He remembered saying to her just recently that he had never worn a condom in their lovemaking, and she had smiled and replied that she was on the pill. Not because she was promiscuous, but it helped to regulate her period, which, when it began, was so heavy it left her exhausted and listless. He wondered if it was a cultural thing with black men, perhaps a hangover from their slavery forefathers who were encouraged to sow their seed as often as possible to increase the slavery stock of their owners. That first time she had wondered why he did not say anything regarding condom protection in their lovemaking, but as she was on the pill, she felt she would not spoil the moment. Subsequent sessions and she took for granted that he knew she was on the pill. When Mercedes had asked him initially to be honest with her in their dealings, she had hoped that opening would give him the chance to tell her about anything before they consummated their relationship. Cane had fathom that but knew that his relationship to Jennifer was over, so, really, there was nothing to tell, and he and Opal had long ceased corresponding after the first few months at Sandhurst.

Cane arrived home with a lot going through his mind. He found Mercedes half asleep as she barely acknowledged his presence. He showered and slipped into bed beside her. She murmured softly and snuggled close to him. Cane did not know if there was an unconscious thought lodged in the innards of his brain dying to get out, but he suddenly found himself saying, as he caressed her slowly, "Mercedes Braithwaite, I really, really love you. Will you marry me?" She shot upright immediately, mouth opened and a startled look on her face.

"What…what?" she gawked, eyes opened wide. "What did you just say?"

"Will you marry me?" Cane repeated.

"Why? What brought this on?" The questions came tumbling out before any answer was given. They spent the next couple of hours discussing the pros and cons, weighing each other aspirations, diversity in culture (although both were from the West Indies), and other aspect of what matrimony would bring. Cane felt good how he was able to answer her questions honestly and truthfully, and she in return expressed her concerns and how they would overcome them. Finally, when he thought perhaps he was wrong to have broach the subject, she pulled him close to her, held him tightly, nibbled his ear, and said, "When?" It was reminiscent of the first time she had done that and said "Be gentle."

As they lay in the afterglow of a different type of lovemaking, one that they shared in separate satisfaction of each other's needs, Cane wondered, *Are there greater heights to ascend, or is this it?* He knew that whatever was happening to him was unique. The word love was magnified a thousand times in his mind, and he sought a definition for it. But none came. He knew for certain that he could never allow anyone to experience what he had found with this woman. The reason why men kill women and women kill men for their spouse had to do with the sharing and the experience that was between the two. Cane knew that asking her to marry him was his way of cementing something that became precious to him. He had no definition for the word love, as there were too many variables depending on what the object of the love was. The emotion that arises when you love a pet, a friend, your parents are close but extremely different.

They both agreed that they would have a simple wedding at the Hammersmith Registry with just a few friends in attendance. Mercedes would invite the three musketeers, and Cane would ask Kendrick Saul to be his best man. The following night, the three musketeers were at the flat when Cane arrived. Mercedes had not told them why she required their presence. As soon as Cane arrived, she told them. For a minute, there was total silence and a look of disbelief on their faces until Megan let out a shriek and ran and hugged Cane. All of a sudden, there was pandemonium as hugs, shrieks, and kisses filled the room. Megan, it was now revealed, had told her other friends that she thought something like that was in the air as her observance of them showed a couple very much in love. They had come to really like Cane, Megan further declared, and even forgave him of being a Jamaican. This brought another round of laughter from all, which suddenly stopped when Megan said, "You are not pregnant, are you?" in a voice mimic of some sitcom TV show actor. Another round of laughter erupted as Mercedes shook her head.

The wedding took place within a week after Cane had proposed, with Megan as her maid of honor and Kendrick as best man. He was given two days off from work when he advised the warden of his intentions, who congratulated him warmly. The warden and his wife and the other two ladies made up the wedding party. Kendrick was totally surprised when Cane broke the news, and for a moment just stared at Cane before pumping his hand and telling him how lucky he was to snare such a brainy, beautiful woman. After the brief ceremony, they retired to the "Forbidden City" Chinese restaurant, where previous arrangements were made for the wedding party. The ambiance was fantastic, and all agreed it was a wonderful "little" wedding. Cane had brought Mercedes a single/dual band; one ring was plain and the other beside it had crushed diamonds. The hundred pounds Batlavala had given him at Sandhurst he had put away for a rainy day came in handy. Mercedes was ecstatic when she saw it and showered him with kisses all over. It might as well be the Crown Jewels for this reward, he joked.

That night as they consummated their marriage, Cane was surprised at the stranger in the bed. If their lovemaking was all consuming and took him to new heights every time, tonight he imagined what it would be like to take LSD, as the lovemaking had risen to the stratosphere and totally blew his mind. *How do you describe perfection?* thought Cane, and the answer came as he lay there, panting.

As if she guessed what was going through his mind, she whispered softly "I am Mrs. Mercedes Braithwaite-Cane now."

She knew that first emotional hurt in Barbados had left a scar, and as she fell hopeless in love with this Jamaican, she had held back just a little, just in case. Tonight, there was no need to, and she gave her all totally and completely.

"Husband," she suddenly said, "you know that from day one you have never told your wife if she was pretty, attractive, or gorgeous or anything flattering, why?"

"Because you are not," Cane said as he turned to face her fully.

"What?" she exclaimed in disbelief.

"Listen, my wife," Cane began. "From the first day I met you and absorbed you in my consciousness as the most defining female I had ever met, I am still searching for the right words to describe you. Since I have not found them yet, I cannot tell you. I am sure as we grow old together, I will find the right words. One thing I do know is that saying you are beautiful, gorgeous, et cetera would not be doing you justice." Mercedes felt her heart swelling and leaned over and kissed her husband gentle on his lips as she snuggled up to share his warmth.

Drifting off to sleep, the thoughts of what had transpired today filled Cane's mind.

It was not just the sex; he knew because many nights they had lain in each other arms, just cuddling and purring and basking with each other without committing the sex act. Yet other times they would exhaust themselves most of the night with repeated lovemaking. The phone rang, bringing both of them to its attention. Mercedes answered and put the speaker phone on. It was her parents.

Megan had told them, on Mercedes' instructions, when they should call because of the time deference between London/Barbados. At first the conversation was strained, with Mercedes assuring them that she was not pregnant and she was okay. After a while, as Cane spoke to Mr. Braithwaite and they found common grounds to explain the scenario, the talk became more jovial. He was an avid cricket fan and so was Cane. The call ended with the promise that as soon as Cane was able, they would visit Barbados, or instead, they would come visit when Mercedes was graduating, which would be in a few months' time. As they lay back, Cane remembered a slightly similar scene when he spoke to his grandmother, and she charged Mercedes to take care of her "one" grandson and wished happiness and prosperity for them both. Cane had sent a letter before to his father outlining his plans. He did not really expect to hear from him just now.

During the past few days the Vietnam War issue was heating up, daily demonstrations outside the US Embassy became fistfights with the anti and pros. Wagonloads of arrests were made daily. Sunday, Cane envisaged that the Metro Police would not have enough vehicles to carry off protesters if John's estimate of the crowd that would be in front of the Embassy was accurate. Cane knew it would.

The Friday August night was hot and humid. Mercedes had called to say she had a special dinner prepared. After the center closed, Cane found himself walking along the Earls Court Road, pondering what his next move in life would be.

He was lost in thought and did not realize that he had strayed from the main road into a short cut alley. He had done it before, so he was not concerned that anything could or would happen. After all, alley or not, Earls Court buzzed with life night or day.

"Hey, kafir, make sure you have your ID card. You know you should not be out at this time of night." Cane whirled around at the voice that had come from behind him. It was unmistakably a South African accent; the term kafir further enhanced that conclusion. There were three of them, all six footers. Cane knew because he was six-two and 170 pounds, and they were all bigger than him. They advanced slowly, each man striking one huge ham-like fist of one hand into the palm of the other. Cane looked ahead; he had about fifty yards to go to the exit of the alley, and behind the advancing men, no other person entered the alley.

They approached one behind the other, but each one slightly ajar to the left of the one in front. The look on their faces, highlighted by the sodium vapor streetlamp, said that whatever they planned was for total enjoyment. The first man actually had a grin on his face as he licked his lips in anticipation of the carnage he was about to unfold. The grin changed to a snarl as Cane unbuttoned his shirt, discarded it, and took up his karate stance in the blink of an eye. The first man rushed him with his left hand held out stiff in front of him and the other hand fist doubled raised high above his head and aimed at Cane's head. On impact, it would more than likely push Cane through the concrete up to about his knees the force he came with. Cane deftly sidestepped, pivoted, and rammed his stiffened toes straight into the man's solar plexus. Cane felt the ribcage give way as a couple of ribs buckled, and the man spat blood and slowly began sinking to the pavement. The kick was followed by a heel crack so powerful behind the knee that it split the patella and hasten his decent into oblivion.

Man number two and three uttered what must be some unmentionable swear words in Dutch but which ended in nigger and charged. Man number two had a young machete (that instrument could never be classified as a knife), so Cane knew he was the danger first. Apparently, white South Africans are used to create mayhem with the over the head profile. Number two had the young machete in his right hand raised high and started to come down with all the strength he could muster. It was either going to split Cane into two or decapitate him from the shoulder. At the same time Cane saw that man number three had bent low, going towards his feet. Cane leaped, catching number two at the axis of the descent of the…okay, knife…and as he landed, swung the man's arm behind his back dislocating the arm at the shoulder. The sound of a thousand different animals dying in agony came from the man. The knife dropped, and he swung his left hand around, catching Cane off balance. Cane fell on his buttocks, and man number three was on him before he could fathom what happened. Man three had him flat on his back but made the mistake of moving forward on Cane chest. Again, the raised hand high above the head aimed at Cane's face. This would probably push his face to the back of his head. As the hand started to descend, man number three never felt the stiffened toes in the shoe once again, that hit him at the base of his neck and the straight fingers that plunge into the larynx. He gurgled a choking sound and rolled over. Number two had retrieved his knife. With the right hand hanging limply, he lurched forward with the knife in his left hand. Cane took a step forward, pivoted on his back foot, and in a sweeping arc, knew as a geri brought the front foot crashing to the side of the attacker's jaw. Incisors, molars, and premolars greeted the policemen who rushed into the alley. Cane had heard the ringing of the police vehicle bells as they grew louder by the second. London police vehicles do not have sirens as there are many World War Two survivors to whom a siren would bring back horrible memories of the German blitz with the V8 rocket on London.

The alley was filled with men in blue in an instant. Cane offered no resistance as they scooped him up and pushed him in the back of a sedan. As they drove off, he noticed that an ambulance had also arrived…bell ringing too…and medics were rushing into the alley.

At the police station, Cane was placed into a small room with a desk and two chairs; one in front and one behind. Nothing was said to him, and as more than an hour elapsed, he began to get a bit anxious. Mercedes would be reaching frantic point by now,, as he had never not called if anything came up and he was going to be late.

His shoes along with the contents of his pockets were removed upon his arrival at the station. He was handed his shirt, which he had discarded before the fight and felt the cold floor through his socks and wondered what the hell was happening. He was just about to start calling out, when the door opened and a man who he imagined to be a plain clothes detective handed him his shoes and mentioned for him to follow. He was led to sedan and hustled into the back seat between two other men like the first. No words were spoken. They turned to face him, and as the car whisked through the almost-deserted London streets, Cane became apprehensive. He had made no contact with Mercedes, and now he was being driven to places unknown by men unknown after an altercation on a London street.

Although the windows were darkly tinted, he realized as the skyscrapers diminished to smaller buildings and, finally, low, separated houses; he was being driven to the outskirts of London. Finally, after about an hour, the car stopped, and he was led into an imposing-looking cottage, even in the darkness that abounded. He surmised that he was in the suburbs, as the houses were far apart and hardly any traffic. Based on the few landmarks he was able to glimpse, he knew that he was heading towards the town of Bromley in the county of Kent. As he followed the first detective up the pathway, he glimpsed one or two ghost-like figures that emerged from the shadows and would quickly disappear again as a signal from the leading man seemed to signify no cause for alarm. Cane's blood pressure at this point must be maxing out because he felt very lightheaded. He was finally led into a very spacious living room-type office. Softly lit, wet bar, glass-top desk, wide cushiony type armchairs, and wall-to-wall carpet. At last, Cane's heart started to slow down. Whatever was going to befall him might not be too unpleasant. This was an Englishman's castle, and nothing foul would blemish it, he thought.

He was ravishingly hungry and soft thud on a table to the side of the wet bar away from him caused him to spin around in time to see a butler type-looking man disappearing down a short corridor. A pot of tea, two chicken club sandwiches, jam, jelly, and some scones were on the tray he had deposited. Cane was not concerned if it was meant for him; a hungry man does not second guess when food is around. So it is drugged… *Well*, he thought, *I needed the sleep*. But it was not, he was on his third cup of tea, having polished off the rest of the contents of the tray, when he heard, "I see you have had a bite," enunciated in the most upper-crust English Etonian accent Cane had ever heard. Only the commandant had Sandhurst came remotely close to this accent. Cane could not believe his eyes when he looked up. Here standing before him at about three in the morning was a man, probably in his late fifties, five-ten to six feet tall, two hundred pounds or so, dressed in a pin-stripe pants, jacket, waistcoat with a carnation in the lapel, bowler hat, and cane. He was indeed drugged. Bowler hat walked over to the desk, placed his cane and bowler on it, and indicated to Cane that he should sit facing him. Cane complied, still in a sort of daze at the man in front of him.

"I am Sir Robert Morley, section chief of MI6 in London. Please sit and listen very carefully to what I have to say without interruption," began Bowler Hat.

"I am called out at this ungodly hour to make a preposition to you, Mr. Cane, that will benefit Her Majesty's Government and you also. Your macho display in the alley at Earls Court earlier will get you some prison time, although you were defending yourself. However, as a Black Belt, I can assure you the Magistrate will find your defense excessive, and you will be sent to prison say for about two to three years." Cane was about to rise and make a protest but was prevented from doing so with a stern, "I said sit and listen without interruption. By the way," he continued, "you were not going to deliver any speech at next Sunday's mass meeting at Hyde Park Corner; you would have been arrested sometime on Saturday on some trump up charge that would necessitate your incarceration. That speech would not go down well with our American cousins. No doubt many would demonstrate outside the courts, protesting your innocence, but that was better than having your inflammatory speech about the Vietnam War broadcast all over England. No, sir, Her Majesty's Government would not allow that to happen." Cane smiled inwardly; no wonder his conversation with the three Peace presidents was taped; one was a phony, a government plant.

The butler appeared with a half-filled brandy glass on a tray and placed it before Sir Morley. He took several measured sips and continued, "The problem was what we could do with you without causing any backlash in certain quarters, apart from the prison thing. Before I go any further, please sign these copies of the Official Secrets Act." Cane hesitated for a minute but knew too well that the smiling Sir Morely before him was even more serious than a judge. He signed where indicated and sat back. "Good," Sir Morley continued. "Your signature here makes you an official agent of HMG, and as such any disclosure you now make pertaining to our discussion here in public will, of course, be denied, and you will rot in some unknown prison." He took another sip of his brandy and continued, "As you know, HMG cannot take sides in the impending civil war that is about to engulf Nigeria. But HMG is on the side that is best suited to the British way of life, and as such will support the Federal Army of Nigeria. We cannot be seen outwardly to be doing this, so we do so through third parties in whatever way best suit the situation." Cane had not noticed before that there was a file on the desk which Sir Morley now thumbed through. "Your gift of oratory, your ability to duplicate accents and pick up languages is noted here in red, Mr. Cane," Sir Morley continued. Cane's mind drift for a moment as he remembered how easily it was for him having heard an accent just a few times to duplicate it, and many thought it was the real McCoy until they saw the face behind the voice. He was especially fond of doing Batlavala Indian accent. He could also converse very quickly in any language he was given the fundamentals and a few hundred most-used words.

The voice of Sir Robert let him refocused. "…will be attached to the Royal Nigerian Army in the rank of a colonel. You will assist in the training their army core in logistics, arms breakdown and assembly, deployment, and tactics. You will not be expected to be active in any actual fighting unless you specifically ask for it."

The last few words were said slower, and Sir Morley fixed him with a steady stare.

He asked Cane if there was anything he wished to have clarified.

"How did MI6 become involved with me from a street fight?" he blurted out.

"Elementary." From his poise and the enunciated word, Cane expected to hear, "my dear Watson," but instead, Sir Morley continued, "A detective recognized you from you TV appearance, and in filing the report, saw your name. A phone call here and a phone call there, and here you are. It was thought it would be an absolute waste to incarcerate a man with your talents for defending himself." The clarification did not help Cane's confused mind, but he said nothing.

He was handed a credit card-sized plastic card with seventeen numbers and the letters FHIG at the end. As he rose from the desk, taking his bowler hat and cane, he said, "You will be enumerated slightly higher that an army captain while you are away and also receive a monthly stipend from the RNA to cover whatever you needs are there. The card you have just been given is a number which you may call from any phone, anywhere, anytime. Please try and store it to memory.

"A story will be put out that you prefer to join the freedom fighters in South Africa, rather than waste your energy denouncing American Imperialism. That should more or less take care of your absence and probably even deflate those who believed in your stance." The door was opened, and as he exited, he said over his shoulder, "The envelope on the desk, please acquaint yourself with its contents, follow its instructions to the tee, and try not to get yourself killed. You have such a lovely wife," and he was gone. It was the first time Cane noticed that he had left an envelope on the desk.

It is not often Sir Morley second-guessed himself. Once he had made a decision based on available data, he tended to be rigid. That is not say he could not be flexible if the situation warranted it. For a brief moment, while addressing the young man who was seated before him, he had what he can only term a very disturbing vision. He had read his file and was very conversant with every aspect of it. But, when he met the real person, file imagery, photos, and reality were not compatible. He saw a very handsome young black man, a tailor's dream in proportional built, bright, brainy and confident; although the latter was an assumption rather than factual. That there was charisma, there was no doubt. He saw Gandhi, Jomo Kenyata, NKruma, Marcus Garvey all rolled into one, and the thought scared him. His brief speech at Speakers Corner galvanized so many people so quickly it was frightening. Sir Morley envisaged that if he was left alone and allow to speak openly about America's involvement in Vietnam, the resulting scenario would cause great discomfort to HMG. Freedom of speech is one thing, but in the hands of this young man, based on the stir he cause in a few minutes, it would indeed be a political fiasco for HMG and her American cousins. He was hoping that by the time Cane came back to England, the war would have been a thing of the past. The civil war in which

Nigeria was headed would not be a short lived one, as previous African unrest had shown, and hopefully, this one would follow previous unrest. Not that he was callous towards the loss of human lives in the bloodletting, but such was the reality of the times we live. There is hardly a nation in history that rose to prominence that did not have their internal wars. The thought that when war came it could be over in the short term meant that was totally acceptable for the return to England of Mr. Cane. In that event, Sir Robert smiled as he thought of the contingency plan that was also in place…just in case.

Cane sat there for what he thought was an eternity, rolling over in his mind the event of the last few hours. Actually it was only a couple of minutes. He stood up, zombie like, and took the brown manila envelope off the desk. He was still contemplating what to do, when the door opened, and the first detective nodded to him to follow. As they exited the cottage, Cane saw that dawn was just breaking. Driving back to London in silence, he was correct in his assumption that they had gone to Bromley in Kent. As they came upon more and more early morning traffic in London, Cane realized that he could not find his way back to that particular cottage on his own.

He still sat between the other two silent men, and as they reached his building in Earls Court, one opened the door, he got out, and they were gone.

Mercedes sat quietly and anxiously by the front window of their first floor flat overlooking the street for the first sign of her husband return. She saw the car pull up and felt her heart began to race as Cane emerged from within. She went quickly to the door and stood just out of reach that when it opened, she would be silhouetted in the doorway. The key entering the locks caused her heart to beat even faster, and then there was Cane. For a brief second, both of them just stood there, then both rushed into each other arms and just held each other tightly. After what seemed like forever, they pulled apart, and the questions came rushing out, in between sobs and hugs from Mercedes.

Cane picked up the manila envelope, which he dropped on entering, and guided his now slightly more composed wife to the settee. He started from leaving the WISC, the fight, taken to the police station and finally to the MI6 cottage and the commitment he had to make to avoid prison here in England.

"No, no," Mercedes exclaime. "We will fight it. My dad will help." The words were coming out fast and furious; she was shaking her head from side to side, sobbing as she comprehended that Cane would be going away. He took her in his arms and tried to console her. He kissed her lips, eyes, cheek, tasted the saltiness of her tears as he tried to reassure her that everything would be all right. He emphasized that the fight fiasco had nothing to do with the government wanting him out of the country; it was his stance, and the potential audience that he might command with his anti-Vietnam crusade.

"What is in the envelope?" she finally asked.

"I don't know. I was waiting until I got home. I suspect it has something to do with my impending travel." It was.

Cane emptied the contents on the center table. They sat down and surveyed its contents. It contained three folder leaves with diverse information on the dos and don'ts of his mission, a micro recorder and tape, plane ticket (for a flight out of Heathrow to Lagos the next afternoon), contact information in Lagos, geographical information on Nigeria, its culture and people. The diesel engine idling of a London taxi just outside their window aroused Cane's curiosity, so he got up and peeked. It could be a visitor to any else in the building. As the person emerged from the taxi, looked up, and saw him at the window, Cane went deadly white. Mercedes saw the change in his frame immediately got up and rushed to the window.

"Who is it, TAC? What is the matter?" she asked anxiously. The taxi had driven off, and the person was out of her sight of vision. "Who is it?" she demanded.

"Jennifer Keller," he said hoarsely.

Before he could answer, the tap on the door told him she was outside his door. There was no need for him to look through the peephole to confirm. He walked slowly to the door and opened it. Mercedes watched him with mixed feelings; she did not know what to expect. As Cane opened the door, Jennifer was on him in a flash, hugging him and searching for his mouth. He was stiff, and she soon realized that something was wrong. As he stepped backwards into the room, Jennifer became aware that someone else was present.

"Jennifer Keller, I presume," said Mercedes in a matter-of-fact manner.

"Thomas, who is this?" Jennifer stammered out.

"Jennifer, meet my wife, Mercedes," said Cane as he emphasized the word wife.

"Your who? Your wife?" Jennifer hardly got the words out.

"Please to meet you. Won't you come in and have a seat," said Mercedes, almost amusingly.

In passing him, Jennifer hesitated for brief moment and looked straight into Cane's eyes with a look on her face that asked the questions how… what… "Why?"

She sat opposite to Mercedes on one end of the settee, and Cane could not help thinking how beautiful she really was. The contrast did not escape him either, two extremely beautiful women, one black and one white.

Cane excused himself to the bathroom. His head was throbbing, and this scenario in his living room was bizarre. As he closed the door, he heard the ending part of a question from Mercedes. "Tell me how long you and TAC were lovers."

Women, he thought.

Jennifer was not an extroverted person, neither was she an inhibited one; but there was something about the young lady in front of her that caused her to speak openly and frankly to her. The image of him on TV at Hyde Park had sparked what she thought was dead, she concluded. From then she made inquiries and traced him to the WISC and, finally, his home address. *Oh Lord,* Merecedes thought, *here is my husband's ex-lover sitting before me, and we are chatting like old friends.* Like Jennifer, Mercedes felt drawn to this attractive white girl and really empathized with her.

"I am really sorry to intrude. I did not know he was married," Jennifer continued.

"I was in London to complete my nursing entrance exam to the Charing Cross Hospital and felt that perhaps I would surprise him. Oh, it was me who was surprised," she said, laughing, and Mercedes joined her.

In a real and funny sort of way, I could be friends with this person, Mercedes thought. Plus she was going into nursing. Another common ground they shared.

Cane emerged from the bathroom, wondering what he was about to face. As he entered the living room, he saw Jennifer and his wife chatting away, and the table was set for three, and they were, in fact, in the kitchen preparing a meal. Cane had not eaten since leaving Sir Morley, and it just dawned on him it was now nearing brunch time, and he was hungry. The scene before him was too weird; he snuck into the bedroom.

In a short while, he heard the call from Mercedes to "come and get it" and came out to a table set with all sorts of goodies, including scones and a steaming pot of tea. He met Jennifer's eyes, and she was smiling. *Memories*, he thought. Throughout the meal there was small talk about this and that and the fact that Jennifer was going into nursing. After the meal, the ladies busied themselves tidying up in the kitchen. Cane sat and watched the events unfolding, totally perplexed.

At long last, Jennifer let out a sight and said, "Thanks for having me here, and please excuse my intrusion." Both ladies embraced.

"Tac, will you walk your friend downstairs? I called a taxi, and I can hear it outside."

Cane was operating on remote mode, and he said, "Of course."

"Well," said Jennifer to Mercedes as she walked towards the door, "you are a very, very attractive and nice person. I could not wish anyone better for Thomas…Tac."

"Thank you," said Mercedes as they embraced one more, "and so are you, Jennifer, a very nice and attractive person also."

Weird, thought Cane as they walked down the stairs in silence. On reaching the exit, Jennifer turned around, looked at Thomas for as few seconds, kissed him on his cheek, said, "All the best to you both," and she was out and into the waiting cab.

On returning to the apartment, Cane did not like the look of mischievousness on Mercedes' face.

"Did you kiss her goodbye?"

"Of course not. What type of question is that?"

"Not even a littlepeck?"

"All right, she kissed me on the cheek…. What is this entire chummy, chummy, friend, friend all-of-a-sudden thing between you two…? What's up?"

"Oh, you are a dope when it comes to women and their emotions. Don't you see that Jennifer really cared for you, perhaps loved you even as much as I do? As soon as I began to talk with her, I felt myself warming towards her. I think she is really the most attractive white woman I have seen since coming to London, and she has a personality to match."

Cane was dumbstruck. He had envisaged a sort of "let me hear your side" question-and-answer session, but here was his wife, actually condoning his previous affair without rancor. He had this nasty feeling that a bombshell was going to be dropped, and he wondered when.

"TAC, why did you not tell me about Jennifer the first time I bared my soul to you?" Mercedees said out of the blue.

"Tell you what? We parted on amicable terms, there was no commitment or promises made, and we did not even keep in touch."

"She is very beautiful and attractive, you think," Mercedes said in mimicry.

Cane was on uncertain ground, whether to agree or disagree. "Yes she is," he finally said.

"Look, my love, I can only confess to something in my past that I think will affect our future; I assure you there is nothing else."

"What about Opal?" she teased.

Cane felt the blood rush to his head, and he felt dizzy. "Oooopal," he stammered,

"Opal," he repeated, more strongly this time.

"Oh, TAC, don't look so bewildered. Your grandmother had called late last night, but I told her you had not come in yet. It was nothing important, she said, just to say hi. We began talking all about your boyhood days, and we gossiped about you girlfriends. Opal's name came up, but I shouldn't worry as there was nothing serious going on, although if you had come back to Jamaica single, she would not mind if you and Opal became serious friends. Opal in the meantime had gotten married to Mr. Bellamy's younger son, Orville, whom you should know, and was getting on with her life. Plus, someone at the WISC had mentioned that they remember seeing you in London some time ago with a really gorgeous white girl, and as soon as I saw Jennifer, I knew it was her." Cane took in all this in silence; he looked intently at the woman before him, held out his arms, and she slipped into them. They headed for the bedroom.

The drive to the Heathrow Airport to catch the flight to Lagos was full of a mixture of laughter, sobbing, hugging, kissing, and promises. The cab driver must have wondered what the dickens was going on. Mercedes was saddened that Cane would not be there for her graduation but had promised to send pictures. She would do at least two more years of specialist nursing to compensate for the time Cane would be away, and more if necessary. Her parents were brought up to speed with what had taken place, and her mom would be joining her soon and remain for as long as she could lend support. Although there could be no direct contact between Cane and Mercedes, she would be appraised from time to time, according to Sir Robert, that he was alive and well. All correspondence to Cane had to be passed to him by way of a post office box here in London. Mercedes was concerned that the war could be a dragged out, one that could last for years and years. Cane assured that after three years, he would find a way to return to her if that was the case. The time could be much shorter, but the maximum was three years.

Although she wanted to be with Cane until the last minute before he stepped onto the plane, Cane preferred their goodbyes in the cab. The kiss was long, deep, and promised a future together. The last thing he saw as the cab pulled away was her gorgeous face in the rear window throwing kisses to him. Cane took a deep breath and stepped into the terminal.

The non-stop flight from Heathrow to Lagos took just over six hours, with one time zone change. Aboard, Cane went over all the material given to him meticulously. He had a window seat in first class, and apart from the initial exchange of greetings by the couple beside him, they soon realized that he preferred to be left alone. The stewardesses, after about three hours into the flight, must have been wondering why this man with the headset kept talking to himself with his eyes closed. In fact, Cane was going over, silently, phrases and words of the most common dialects in Nigeria. The micro recorder with the different playback dialects was indeed a helpful tool. A snack was served shortly after takeoff, and he was informed that dinner would now be served. They were about two hours before landing in Lagos. After dinner, Cane did not know when he drifted off to sleep and was surprised when he was gently awakened to fasten his seat belt as they were about to land. He was not fully awake or focused and sat upright quickly, quickly enough to startle the stewardess who apologized for waking him up, but she said regulations stipulated that all passengers be awake for landing. Cane smiled and he apologized, as, in his half-awakened state, the face leaning over him to awake was that of Jennifer Keller.

Inside Lagos International it was bevy of activity with a lot of military personnel going to and fro. It was very crowded, but not chaotic. He was listed as a businessman in his British passport and cleared Customs and Immigration without any trouble.

Exiting the main lobby, he saw the card, "Thomas Cane," being held by a young man in an evening suite. Cane went over, identified himself, and the man took his travel case, introduced himself as Corporal Effyong, and invited Cane to follow to the car parked in the No Parking area.

As they drove off, Cpl. Effpoyon informed Cane that he was assigned to him for the duration of his stay in Nigeria and was now heading to the Lagos Regency Hotel, where a two-bedroom suite was held for him. His name was difficult to pronounce, and as such, he was referred to as Effy. That would also be his place of abode while in Lagos. He was due to meet with army generals at Army headquarters at ten a.m. tomorrow, and he would pick him up at nine. Although the headquarters was only fifteen minutes away from the hotel, he was told to pick up at nine.

An overtaking car coming from the opposite direction caused Effyon to swerve violently to avoid a head-on, and as he righted the car, he swore in Arundi, the common dialect.

"I don't think his mother is such a lowly animal," Cane said, as the Corporal got the car under full control.

Effyon's mouth opened wide for a few seconds as if trying to say something until finally he said, "You understand Arundi."

"A little," Cane said, smiling. They drove in silence and without further incidence to the hotel. Again, the car was parked in a No Parking area. Cane surmised that the license plate letters and numbers said, "Do not touch."

At the reception desk, he was given a warm welcome by an attractive receptionist, whose disposition and attire reminded Cane of a proper English school marm at a boarding school. He signed a paper and was given key card and a folder. As he turned away, with Effyong following closely, the receptionist said, "He is handsome, Effy," she said in Arundi, to the discomfort of Effy who figured Cane would have heard that remark.

As soon as he had settled in, had some breakfast sent up, he asked for an outside phone line, got out his M16 card, and called London. There were tweets and beeps, and to his surprise, a voice said, "Yes, Mr. Cane, can I help you?"

Cane was speechless for a second or two. "Y…yes, I would like to be connected to Mrs. Cane."

"Before we do that, Mr. Cane," the voice continued, "what do the letters FHIG on your card stand for?"

Cane's mind raced. FHIG…FHIG…he was never told by Morley. As he pondered the answer, it became obvious that the line had gone dead. Apparently if you could not answer that question, then the voice at the other end assumed it was not a genuine caller using the card. With some trepidation, he redialed; the same voice answered and asked the same question. "Fitzhenly Institute for the Gifted," Cane blurted out. It was a wild guess but was the only one he could think of.

"Thank you," said the voice. "I will connect you now." Cane heard the distant ringing of the phone and held his breath in anticipation when Mercedes would answer. His breath came out slowly as he realized that she would never let the phone ring so long without answering. "Sorry," said the voice, "there does seem to be anyone at home. You will have to try your call later, and please remember the time difference." Cane hung up very slowly; he would try later, about four p.m. his time when it would be about eight or nine in London. He sat down on the bed wearily and stretched out. He was awakened by the ringing of the phone, and on answering, it was Nana, the receptionist, asking if he would be having dinner. Glancing at the clock, he saw that it was eighty-thirty p.m. Bolting upright, he asked for an outside line and made the call to London with the same results. Where was Mercedes? Surely, after midnight she should be home.

As soon as he hung up, the phone rang. Again, it was Nana. He apologized for hanging up and said he would come down for dinner. She explained that she was off duty some time ago but came to the hotel most evenings for dinner and the disco afterwards if she felt like it. He felt refreshed, having slept for over eight hours. His closest contained five well-pressed RNA uniforms with the captain insignia. He tried one on, and it fit perfectly. He assumed the others were identical replicas, so they, too, would fit. He did not fancy wearing army fatigues to dinner, so, after showering, he dressed casually and went down to the dining hall. Nana was standing near the entrance, and at first he did not recognize her, as her transformation from receptionist to diner was absolutely mind blowing. She smiled and said, "Hello, Captain Cane," as he acknowledged, and they both went into the dining room. Once seated and order placed, they began small talk. Cane realized that from her overheard remark earlier and the way she looked now, he could be very vulnerable. He steered the conversation to his inability to get through to his wife in London and observed her keenly while he spoke. The mention of his wife and reminiscing about her did not seem to have any visible or oral effect as Nana continued to ask every now and then about Mercedes. "When will she finish nursing? Are you going to have children?" et al.

After dinner, Cane was invited to the disco to "shake a leg," as Nana put it. Cane reminded her that he would not stay long as he wanted to be at his peak tomorrow when he meets army brass. Cane moved easily to pulsating rhythms and watched Nana as she really let herself go, with a mischievous smile on her face at all times. When they danced close up, Cane could feel her body melting into his, her arms around his neck and every so often moving her face so that her lips would brush his slightly, but never stopping.

Cane did not know how long this war would last, and here was Nana, an apple ripe for the picking, which Eve did not resist, but he would. He reasoned that any involvement so early would only complicate his life even further. At about eleven p.m., Cane hinted that he felt the jet lag creeping in, and he would prefer to retire. He could see the disappointment on Nana's face, but she smiled and said, "Okay… Tomorrow is another day," kissed him on the cheek as they exited the disco room. He watched as she went out, and a taxi pulled up before he pressed the elevator button for his floor.

The next morning, he was having breakfast in the dining room when he saw Effy by the elevator. It was eighty-fifty a.m. He signaled him to come over and finish breakfast by having a cup of coffee. Cane was ready at precisely nine a.m., and with Effy's nod, they arose and walked out towards the front entrance. Cane passed Nana at the reception desk and stopped for a brief moment to take in the transformation before him. She was dressed like the "school marm" outfit she had portray the day before. She smiled and winked at him as he passed. He returned the smile and wink.

The drive to army headquarters was uneventful, as far as Cane was concerned. After two near what he thought were certain death encounters, he had closed his eyes for the rest of the trip. His blood pressure and heart rate were not accustomed to these leaps and accelerated movements. By closing his eyes, he preferred not to see, not only his own near misses of certain death but others. There was no way he believed that the death rate in Lagos alone did not run into double fugues on a daily basis through traffic accidents.

The imposing building at the army headquarters read, "Military Headquarters," and served the army, navy, and Air Force. After passing through a couple of checkpoints, with Effy flashing some sort of badge, they arrived. He was ushered into a lavishly furnished lounge and told to wait until summoned at precisely ten a.m., and an orderly came and escorted to double doors, which after knocking and hearing "Enter," he was shown into another lavishly furnished room with a huge table, which, quickly counting, seated twelve. He saluted and was acknowledged. Sitting at the head of the table was Brigadire General Kipsume. Cane knew all of them from his briefing and photos that were in the manila envelope. Kipsume was the supreme commander of all the military branches. As he outlined what Captain Cane role was to be and all the ramifications that full cooperation would entail, Cane overheard General Assawabe, who was sitting next to him, telling another general that they, meaning the English, had sent a boy to do a man's job, like David and Goliath. The message was passed around, and as each general that got it would smile and shake his head. After the briefing, which lasted just over an hour, General Kipsume rose took his salutes and terminated the meeting. All the other generals rose and began chit chat among themselves, nodding to Cane, wishing success etc. Cane thanked them all in English, and as he saluted to leave, said in Arundi, "Yes but David slew Goliath." The silence that followed surpassed deafening as each general looked at each other. And, as if orchestrated, they all burst out laughing as Cane reached the door, which the orderly was opening. As he emerged, Effy, who was standing to one side, rushed over with anxiety on his face, asking, "What happened…what happened?" Most of the generals were emerging still laughing. In the car, Cane told Effy what transpired, and he, too, began to laugh.

The rest of the day was spent with Cane going from unit to unit, meeting with army personnel, explaining the how, what, where, and why his schedule would follow, and, most of all, expectations. Cane did not know how he did it, but somehow, Effy had let out that remarks in dialect, especially disparaging ones, could be understood by the captain. On several occasions he was asked in dialect a question pertaining to his work.

His last stop was a huge warehouse workshop which had been set up to accommodate the training schedules of the different units. Cane sighed as he rested in the rear of the car as Effy made his way back to the hotel. He was exhausted, and he had not yet really started.

Cane closed his eyes, and his mind wandered to the several attempts he had made to try and get in touch with his wife. From time to time, he would hear Effy swearing under his breath as the car swerved. He had tried three times today, and each time the result was the same. They were so exact that he began to suspect that he was listening to a tape. He would try a different tactic later.

He did not see Nana at the desk as he passed and suspected that she was off duty. As he made his way to his door, he wondered where she lived, if it was close by, did she have a car, how did she get home the other night? So lost in thought that he had passed his door and had to back pedal.

Inside, he showered, causally dressed; dinner was some time off, so he decided to go over the mountain of paperwork he had accumulated during his acquaintance journey around army headquarters. A cold beer from the fridge helped him as he leafed through the paperwork. After completing his preliminary look through, he realized that he had to strategize concretely how he was going to tackle his job. He also aware that the war at this point was at a stalemate in terms of which army had the upper hand. Lack of complete logistics, on both sides, resulted in ground won today would be yielded the next. He sighted heavily to his mind the best description of what was taken place was one step forward, two steps back. It was almost eight p.m., one a.m. in London. Cane went through the phone routine, but instead of saying "Can I speak to Mrs. Cane?" he said, "Can I speak to the Prime Minister or a cab driver?" Without hesitation, he was asked the same questions, but he noticed that just before he said cab driver, the phone began to ring. He heard the familiar ring of a telephone, and just as he suspected, after the eighth ring, the voice came back to repeat just as before. As Cane hung up the phone, a deep sense of despair came over him. He was abandoned by Her Majesty's Government for whatever reason. He had assumed that he had a round-trip ticket and initially did not check; he did so now, and was not surprised that it was one way.

The ringing of the telephone awoke him, and glancing at the clock, he saw that it was just about ten-thirty. He had fallen asleep with the ticket in his hand as some sort of further body blow, which knocked him out. It was Nana on the line. No, she was not at the hotel, her shift had ended, and she would be doing ten to six for the next two week as of tomorrow. She was not certain what time he got in and just wanted him to know in case he was wondering what had happened to her. He tried to sound cheerful as he told her he would stay in touch. As he hung up, he wondered if she read anything in his voice. Calling down for a late snack, he decided to take stock of his position and any ramifications that he could foresee.

1. His joint account in London would be credited with two hundred and eighty pounds on the first of every month.

2. His sojourn in Nigeria was covered by the Nigerian Government, who paid for his stay at the hotel and all meals.

3. His worn uniforms would be collected on Saturday mornings and returned Sunday evening.

4. He had a bank card for the Lagos International Bank, where the equivalent of one hundred and forty pounds would be credited to his account every month

5. He had a British passport that was valid for the next ten years.

Cane looked over the list and felt a bit better in his mind. He knew that Mercedes would not be cash short, she had her pay as well, plus if it came down to the wire, she had her parents to fall back on. As he visualized a scenario where Mercedes managed to inquire about his wellbeing, she would get neither a positive nor negative reply. She would get something in the order of, "He was last seen alive in X Provence a few days ago." If he happened to die in between those inquires, she would then be informed. Basically, he knew that for the duration of the war, he would be staying put; it was logical and financially viable for him to do so. Dealing with the emotional separation with no contact from Mercedes he had to overcome in his own way.

As the weeks turned into months and the months to years, Cane threw himself into his work. Most weekends away from work, he would just take long walks, semi tours of the city, and plan. It was obvious that his planning and attention to details were paying off from as early as three months from his planning logistics, for the different combat units generals were showering compliments on him. General Assambyo, whose offensive captured one of the largest towns in the Eastern Provence, was one of the most complimentary. Not only did his troops capture, and held, the town but were able to repulse with devastating effect a counterattack by a full Biafarian brigade. Initially, when Cane drew up the logistics in the offensive, the General was not too enthuses as he had gone through something similar earlier with heavy losses and defeatist moral from his troops. He could not believe how the arrival of food, gasoline, ammo, replacement parts, and causality withdrawal and replacement troop went so smoothly. Of course, not all units had the immediate success like General Assamby, but as time wore on, victories, holding, advancing became the norm for the RNA.

In the early days, Cane had very little time for socializing. Apart from the earlier encounter with Nana, dinner and disco, it was about two months before they made contact again. On a trip to a boutique for the fashion conscious in Akeje, an hour's drive from Lagos, Cane was coming out Myumba Boutique, when someone crossing the street caught his attention. He stood and watched her as the cars navigate around her, rather than she doing the navigating. As she reached the sidewalk, she looked up and saw him. For an indefinite second, which was like an hour, neither said anything, and the invisible starter gun in both their heads popped at the same time, and they moved into each other's arms in a tight embrace. Cane had only fleeting glimpse of her over the last few months, and never enough time to exchange words. Pouring his heart into his work and the dullness that envelope him from his non-contact with Mercedes had left him sort of anti-social. Breaking the embrace, her questions came so rapidly both in English and Arundi. Cane smiled as he steered her to a table roadside cafe and sat down. Both of them ordered a refreshing limeade, as the day was very hot and it was a cold, refreshing drink. As she sipped her drink, she kept looking at him, smiling. Finally, they were able to converse. She knew Cane was still at the hotel, and she, too, was now the assistant manager, with her own flat on the tenth floor. Similar to what Cane had. She had not called Cane because he had promised to call her the last time they spoke, but she said that based on how he sounded, she knew it was just a put off. Cane was able to tell her why he sounded that way and how things at the army were going. She was in Akeje to visit relatives, just to make sure they were all right. In this war, you never know. Effy did not provide Cane with transport on weekends, and he had taken a taxi, much to the delight of the cabby when he told him where he wanted to go. Nana said that she was about to leave and asked, if he wanted, her car was in the car park just around the corner, and it was no problem giving him a lift as they were going in the same direction. The last few words came out with a wide smile. Cane paid the bill, and they got up and began walking. After a few strides, it occurred to him that he had not left a tip. Excusing himself, he returned to the table where the waiter was still standing, watching them depart. From where Nana was standing, she saw the waiter's face broke out into a large smile as Cane handed him something. Cane turned and saw Nana standing there elegantly. She looked breathtaking in a tight-fitting blouse and mini skirt that highlighted her amble body curves that were proportionally matched from head to toe.

He felt a slight rush of blood in his loins, but managed to control the rising upsurge as he took her arms to cross the road.

The drive back was full of chit chat, and every chance he got, Cane spoke in Arundi. As they reached the outskirts, Cane found himself asking her a lot of personal questions. The one important one was, being so attractive, how come she was not married, or, he assumed, perhaps incorrectly, that she did not have a steady guy. She smiled broadly and broke into a laugh. "I just have not seen or found anyone that I wanted to go steady with. Most of the good, eligible men are in the military, and the rest are not up to my academic standard or earning potential." The chit chat continued until they pulled into the car park at the hotel. As they alighted, she said, "It's still early. Why don't you come up to my apartment and let me cook you a real Nigerian dinner?"

Cane said yes without hesitation and went up the service elevator to her apartment. It was just like Cane's, but it had a well-equipped kitchen. Cane knew that she could easily ordered from the hotel kitchen, but memories of an almost similar encounter were ticking over in his brain, and he wondered if it would end the same.

Invited to make himself at home after a really cold of lager was offered, she disappeared into the bathroom. The vista from the tenth floor overlooking the city was not all that attractive, as several taller buildings obscured any real view that was out there. More than likely, management placed senior staff in this area instead of guests to minimize complaints from guests. After wondering around a bit, Cane saw a Bob Marley LP and placed it on the turntable nearby. A set of headphones completed the setting. His back was turned away from the kitchen, and after listening to a few tracks, his beer was also finished. He got up and headed for the kitchen and could not help smiling as he saw Nana and thought she was imitating a bee with her movements as she reached for a number of things to assist her with her cooking. She saw his empty glass, nodded to the refrigerator, and smiled. Cane noticed that she had on a one-piece traditional dashiki dress, but this one was close fitting, instead of the loose. She twisted and turned in reaching for condiments, and he smiled to himself as he refilled his glass; it was obvious that she was not wearing a bra.

Cane settled down to listen with his headphones, and just as he was about to rise again, having taken off the headset, he heard, "Come and get it." Looking at the set table before him, he could hardly believe his eyes. Several dishes adorned the table, candle, and a wine bucket. Nana had also changed as her hair now was encased in a wrap; the material matched the mini dashiki she also changed into. Pouring her wine, they clink glasses and began to eat. He sampled everything before him and learned their names: Jello rice, dodo, moon moon, a.k.a. ma, and many more as he went along. Finally, he was sated. Looking around, almost every plate was empty. She had prepared almost to the absolute degree enough for two. Cane thought she must have gauged his appetite from their first dinner. They moved to the settee after everything was placed in the dishwasher. Anyone entering the apartment would not be able to tell that a mini feast was just concluded. Bob Marley was still wailing away, and careful not to spill her wine, she nestled into his shoulder.

"Tell me, Mr. English-Jamaican, about your country" she said softly.

The wine, the food, the everything was too much for Cane. Her lips pressed hard against his, and she searched for his tongue. For a brief second, he hesitated, then it was all over. He felt the hardness of her nipples rising as he pulled her closer, and she reciprocated hungrily as they began to undress. All his pent-up emotions came to the fore as he pressed harder and harder into her. The tightening of her hands around his neck and the violent trembling of her body told him told him that she had climaxed almost at the same time he did. It was more like a physical release for both of them, rather than lovemaking. She slowly arose, took his hand, and led him into the bedroom. He followed by reflex rather than his brain telling him to go and slid into the bed beside her as she reached for him once more. The thought that he was not wearing a condom did not seem to be a concern at the moment.

That night marked the beginning of a relationship that was more physical than loving. Many times, in the afterglow of sex, they spoke about their relationship without mentioning love for each other. She was on the pill, she told Cane, and hoped that although she had no claims on him, he would deal with her alone as she would be only dealing with him. Deja vu, thought Cane. He knew he had strong feelings for her but felt inhibited in expressing them; mainly because what he knew he had with Mercedes. Nana cared deeply, too, but was always aware that sometime in the future he would be gone. Although the hotel was huge, he had no doubt that through the maid service grapevine, their relationship was not a secret. They interchanged sleeping arrangements, depending on what they were doing or where they were before returning to the hotel. Toothbrush, panties, hairbrush, men's underwear were just a few of the telltale signs in either apartment. Nana would join Cane from time to time as he practiced his aerobics to stay in shape and giggled as he often broke into his Taekwondo Kata and the utterances he would make as he completed his moves.

The weeks rolled into months, and then to years, and Cane spent all of his spare time with Nana. The only cloud was Cpl. Effy. He noticed that a few weeks after he and Nana had consolidated their relationship, Effy became very aloof in their interactions. Although a corporal, Cane had dispensed with salute every time they met and had discussed a variety of topics as they interacted. Effy reverted to saluting while in uniform, and their drives mornings and evenings were mainly silent. Cane had tried to casually find out what the matter was but met with a "mind your own business" attitude. After a few attempts to placate their indifferences, Cane let it go. Cane wondered if it had anything to do with Nana and told her of what was transpiring with Effy. She said that she had dated him a few times casually without intimacy as he frequented the hotel with other foreigners that the Nigerian Government Accommodated. However, she stopped, she said, when she realized that he wanted the relationship to go further. Dinner at the hotel, about once every four weeks or so, was the limit of their encounter the past few months.

As the RNA took hold of previous occupied township, their drives into countryside became longer, but Cane always made sure that his Uzi was set on automatic and was by his feet. The war was winding down, and Cane knew that in a very short while the Biafrans would surrender. They did just that by late December 1970. The war was over. The day before, he had asked General Assembly if he could go on one of the mop-up patrols to outlying areas where communication was fragile to get those who did not hear the official ceasefire that the war was over. His request was granted, and the experience of what he saw in barbarism, cruelty, and inhuman behavior caused him to tune out of trying to understand what made man behave the way he did to his fellow man. The German-Jewish experience, the Vietnam War, and the atrocities that were chronicled made him wonder what was behind leaders thinking in committing the things they did. There was no other Earth; we were all on this one together. We came and saw it, and we would die leaving it. Man should and will die for many things, but politics should not be one of them. It was too easily duplicated to suit those who wanted something greater than to control lives. Cane was lost in thought, when a violent lurching catapulted him into the men seated on the other side of the personnel carrier. He landed on caught-his-penis-in-his-zipper and could not help smiling when he remembered the howl that escaped his throat. The smile changed quickly to one of contempt as he also remembered what he was about to do. Looking through the windshield, Cane saw that they were pretty close to Army Headquarters, and further quick lurches of the vehicle confirmed, yes, they were in Lagos.

Cane picked up an envelope from his cubby hole in the hotel. It bore the stamp and seal of the RNA, and as he waited for the elevator, he slit it open. Reading as entered and exited the elevator for his apartment, the contents were not totally unexpected, but he was surprised at its swiftness. In essence, the letter said that as of the end of DEC, his stipend would cease, his uniforms removed, and his room no longer would be paid for by the RNA. He could stay at his own expense or seek alternative accommodation. The rest of the letter was thanking him for his contribution and the report that would be sent to London. As he closed his apartment door, a "Is that you, Cane?" came from the bedroom. Nana was relaxing, watching TV. As he changed clothes, for the last time getting out of his captain uniform, he tossed the letter to Nana. She read without saying anything, and, at the end, just placed the letter on the night table, turned, and invited him into her arms. He was in his undies at this time of his undressing, and as he lifted the sheet, he saw that she was naked.

"When are you leaving?" she said in pillow talk after they had one of the best lovemaking sessions, Cane thought. "Why do you have to leave?" she continued before Cane could answer. "You could move in with me; my contract allows for a spouse." Cane indicated to her to be silent, and took up the phone, asked for an outside line, and dialed his favorite number. She watched in amazement as he mimed the procedure. After a few moments after speaking, she watched him count to eight then hung up.

"Nana, I can't give you an answer just now. Let me unravel some things first. I promise I should by tomorrow." She nodded and got up. Showering together, they planned to go to a movie and a Chinese restaurant later. Before leaving, Cane called British Airways and was told he had to come in person to the airport to book a flight, as departing passengers were prioritized.

Nana was on duty early the next morning, and as she left her apartment, she smiled and said, "Drive carefully," as she tossed the keys to her Volvo 323 to him. There would be no Effy at nine a.m., Cane thought as he showered, shaved, and then made his own breakfast. The drive to the airport was to take about forty-five minutes. But Cane entered the highway behind an ever so long line of traffic that seemed to move about three car lengths every five minutes. He was glad, in one respect, as he was not in a hurry, and with less traffic, he would have had to be avoiding some sort of collision continuously. He crept along like this for two hours until finally he was in front of the main terminal building. It was obvious no one adhered to parking signs, so as soon as he saw a slot, he squeezed in, just ahead of another motorist who swore that his mother was a jackal and his father a hyena. Cane smiled and replied in Arundi, "The same to you." Cane watched the look of astonishment come over the man's face. Cane's complexion was a few shades lighter than the average Nigerian, and out of uniform, he had to be a misguided tourist. A mercenary or from a tribe that just lost the war.

The line to the airline counter was also long but moved quickly as there were quite a few customer representatives dealing with the queue. At the counter, Cane handed in his passport as requested and watched as she scanned through several letter-sized papers containing numbers. As she did so, Cane asked when he would be able to get on a flight. She looked up and informed him that if his passport number was on the list, about three weeks; unfortunately, it was not, so it would be anywhere between two to three months. Nigeria Air and British Airways were the only two airlines flying directly to London on a every other day basis. There were other airlines going all over Europe, which he could try then try to link from some other city to London, she informed him. There were three other international airlines, and Cane spent the rest of the day trying to get information if he could get a flight out of Nigeria. He picked up snippets of information as he wandered around the terminal, and apparently, all foreigners were trying to get out as quickly as possible in case there were repercussions meted out to those who helped the Biafrans. Over a thousand different mercenary nationalities were present in Nigeria, and one could not distinguish which side each took.

Cane arrived back at the hotel carpark late. The drive back from the airport took just as long as going. Not because of a long line of traffic, but Cane drove very slow and watchful and suffered the lowest forms of swearing indignities from other irate drivers. Nana's usual parking place was occupied, and he found another almost in the unlit rear of the parking lot. He was tired and hungry and envisaged a hot shower and a juicy steak to pep him up. He was lost in thought as he alighted and began to lock the door. Out of the corner of his eye, he caught the shadow of a huge man that was almost upon him in the door glass. He slid sideways, ducked, and pivoted, unleashing a kick to the man's kneecaps and heard the cracking of broken bones as the man slumped to the ground, clutching his knee and howling in agony. He was between cars and saw two more approaching from either side. They also were huge. Contemplating his next move, the decision was taken away as two more leapt on top of the cars on either side. In the melee that followed within the cramp spaces, he was holding his own until he felt something like a sandbag hit him flush on the forehead, scattering his equilibrium, then a pole like hit into his solar plexus, and he went down. Kicks and blows followed him to that resting place, and just before he passed out, he heard in English, "Stay away from Nana."

Cane arose coming from a very, very far place in his mind; he felt a sort of softness beneath him and smelled something closely akin to disinfectant and heard voices. He slowly opened his eyes and was aware that he could only see clearly out of one. As his mind began to put reality together, he concluded that he was in a hospital bed, and there were two nurses around doing what nurses do to patients like him. He was fully conscious, focused, and tried to smile as Nana entered the room. She came over, and not knowing how fragile he was, embraced carefully in his prone position. Holding back tears, she just kept saying, "Oh Cane… Oh Cane.

After a while, still aching, he was propped up, and Nana related the events from the carpark. He was concussed, badly beaten, with no broken bones. Sprains yes, but nothing broken. Apparently, the lack of space between the cars had prevented his attackers from really laying it into him. A resident looking for parking space saw what was happening and made an alarm. The attackers ran off, and an ambulance was summoned. At the Lagos General Hospital, a beaten-up stranger arriving in Emergency was no big thing; he would have to wait his turn to be attended. Thankfully, from the outbreak of war, military personnel were shunted to the base hospital camps. That move, however, made the LGH very short staffed. She had gone to his room when she came off duty, wondering where he was, and decided to pack his things to take to her apartment, which she did. As she left the elevator, she overheard a conversation by two residents about the man who was attacked in the car park. Out of curiosity, she inquired, as a hotel staff, and was told where. Arriving at the spot, she saw her car with the keys still in the lock and rushed over to the

LGH. She saw him lying on a stretcher in the emergency room. She knew key members of staff at the hospital, and retrieving his passport from his pocket to identify him, quickly got him to one of the last private rooms left, where he was seen and examined by a doctor and X-rayed. She smiled, leaned over, and kissed him on his swollen lips.

Cane related his ordeal at the airport and his late arrival at the carpark. He wondered if he should reveal what he heard before passing out. "Cane, I know Effy and his men were responsible," she blurted out, with tears running down her face. "I did not think he still had a thing for me after all this time, but according to him, he did, and now that the war is over, if you did not leave, he is going to make sure you do."

Cane reached for her hand, held it, and tried to exert some pressure to let her know he cared. "Nana, Efffy and his thugs could not force me to leave if I wanted to stay. But until I know what has happened in London to Mercedes, I would never be truly yours. I have to try and get back." She nodded and returned his squeeze.

Although there were no broken bones, there was a lot of bruising and swelling. It took ten days for Cane to feel truly fit, and the doctor, after running him through some physical and mental tests, released him. During that time, Nana visited him every day and brought him up to date as to what was happening in Nigeria. All borders were closed to neighboring countries, and a lot of curfews. Supreme Commander Kipsume wanted his pound of flesh. Many RNA soldiers had deserted to join the Biafran army based on their ethnic origin, and many Biafrans who were in the Nigerian government had left their jobs. Kipsume was making sure that he would get them if they tried to sneak out of the country or were hiding. Nana told Cane Effy was promoted to lead a military intelligence unit.

Nana came for him on the day of his discharge, and as they drove back to the hotel, she advised him that he should clean out his account, as there was turmoil in the banking system with Biafran dollars as plentiful as genuine Nigerian dollars. The Nigerian government had not yet made a definable proclamation on the status of the B/dollar, but she heard that they were going to be depreciated almost to five percent of its value against the N$. It was mid-morning, and by the time he got through at the bank it was midafternoon. He had his account changed to U$, and left with about $14,000.00

He was surprised that he had so much, but over the past three years, he had spent very little in socializing on himself.

The continuing drive back to the hotel was spent in very little chit chat, and Cane suspected that there was something troubling her which she was not saying. In the apartment, she ordered lunch, and after they had eaten, she disappeared into the bathroom. In the bedroom closet, Cane saw his clothes were laid out and personal toiletries placed on a shelf. The closing of the door behind caused him to turn around. Nana was wearing just a see-through gown with nothing underneath. Silently and wordlessly, she came over to him and began to undress him. The aroma of her bath oils and perfume was intoxicating. She literally threw him on the bed, when he was naked, and his manhood raised. The sex that followed was mind blowing to Cane. She was all over him, up, down, around, panting, pulling, squealing, and moaning as she burst into a tremendous climax. They lay there for a while, until the pace of their breathing slowed to normal.

Without asking, Cane knew that this last sex was a "goodbye" act. "Cane, I am really, really sorry," she finally said. "But you must leave Nigeria tonight. Effy gave me a ticket for a SWISS charter flight out of Ikeja at nine p.m. It is controlled by the RNA, and only European nationals that the NA can verify will be on it. He has assured me that you will be okay." She did not pause while giving Cane the info, as if she wanted to get it off her chest, and he knew then that was why she was a bit silent from the hospital to the hotel. "Cane," she said, "without an NRA uniform, walking around Lagos you will be a target for mugging or possible killing; there would be an assumption, especially by NRA soldiers, that you were a Biafran mercenary trying to blend." Cane nodded, reached for her, and gave her a long, lingering kiss, which she reciprocated as soon as he paused. He could sense the passion rising again, but gently eased away from her. She gave him the ticket, which he scrutinized and saw that it was a one-way ticket to Bern in Switzerland. With his British passport, Cane could not envisage any problem he would having getting a flight to London.

His duffle army bag from London, which was placed into his suitcase, had a secret compartment. He discarded the suitcase and told Nana, who had gone out into the kitchen, that he would just use the bag as he only had a few pieces of clothing etc. Except for a few thousand dollars he placed the large bank notes in such a way that only an expert in this type of scrutiny of luggage, examining the bag would be able to detect that something was there. Nana said it would take just over an hour or so, based on the traffic, to get to the airport, so they should leave at about seven p.m. Cane agreed and continued to pack as she entered the room with a cold beer. After packing, they sat in the lounge, drinking and reminiscing. Soon, it was time for him to leave. He showered and dressed in jeans and long-sleeved shirt. He had no idea what Bern weather was like at this time of the year but would cross that hurdle when he reached it if the weather was cold. Strapping on a money belt, which he had also retrieved from his duffle bag, he gave Nana the impression that was where his funds from the bank were hidden.

The ride to Ikeja was almost like the ride from the hospital to the hotel, very little was said. The road was crowded with people, animals, and all manner of transport as people made their way either to or from where they were displaced during the war. She blew her horn continuously, adding that she hardly drove in the rural areas as the road was clogged with refugees going or coming. Finally, but on time, she turned into a large expanse of land with many buildings and aircraft parked at various points. Almost immediately, they were stopped by RNA soldiers. Nana handed some papers, and after checking them, he waved her on, indicating where she should go.

Nana drove to the main terminal building and stopped before one of the entrance doors. Cane could see inside that there were about fifty to sixtyer persons there of mainly European descent milling around, and one of two Middle Easterners. As he opened the car door, Nana reached over and kissed him on the cheek, telling him to write to her at the hotel when he was settled. Cane said he would but knew within his heart that this was a chapter in his life that ended here. She blew him a kiss and drove off.

Cane was searching for somewhere to sit, when two soldiers approached ask for his ticket, then asked him to accompany them to a small office at the far end of the room. Entering the office, it was empty except for two chairs and a desk. The two soldiers had mentioned for him to enter but stood by the door. In a short while, Effy entered with the two soldiers who took his duffle bag and began to methodically search it by removing everything and opening them up. Cane was still standing as Effy sat and began to tell the soldiers to pat him down carefully, stopped, and started to smile. Their eyes met, and Effy's smile became broader as he was aware that Cane understood whatever he was saying. He switched to Igbo, and Cane replied, "I know that, too," in Ibo. A silence, then Effy said in English, "Mr. Cane, are you carrying any large sums of money out of Nigeria in whatever currency?" Cane saw that the two soldiers were repacking his bag after emptying and shaking it and indicated to Effy his money belt.

He unbuckled it and handed it to him. Cane showed him how it was opened and revealed ten US one-hundred-dollar bills. Effy stood for a moment, looking at the money, and literally spat out, "That's all?" Cane said that his money was sent by standing order every month to his account in London as he had very little need of cash while on assignment to the RNA. It was a lie, and Cane knew that if Effy had information to the contrary, it would be disclosed now. After scratching his head, he handed the belt back to Cane, less five hundred USD, and told him he will need five hundred dollarsto get to London.

Cane started to protest as why his five hundred dollars was taken. Effy just smiled and said it was for the ticket and left the office. Cane knew that if he had not hidden his money, he would have been relieved of it also.

The flight was called, and after showing his ticket to the two soldiers at the exit door, he boarded the plane. It was a Turbo Pro Twin US Embrace, seating one hundred, with a crew of five. The five- to six-hour journey would be dreary, noisy, and bumpy, as these types of planes were more prone to weather variances. Cane settled down beside a Frenchman named Jacques, or so he said, no surname, and introduced himself. It was obvious to Cane from the little talk that took place among the passengers that most of them were strangers to each other and were not prepared to give any information about themselves that was not necessary. The Swiss were always neutral in a war but who knows to whom one was talking. As the lights of Lagos disappeared, Cane settled down with a French disc he had inserted into his micro cassette and began to revise his French. Most of Europe spoke French, and he knew the Swiss did. He also had Italian/German and Spanish disc, which he had obtained at the airport kiosk in London before leaving.

Three hours into the flight, a meal was served, which he ate slowly while pondering about the experience at Ikeja with Effy. He had asked Jacques if he was searched or asked about money, and he had replied negatively on both questions. Cane told him that he was and wondered why. Cane knew that somehow Nana and Effy had worked out their differences, and it was she who had suggested that he withdrew his money. She had not seen it, nor did he disclose how much. It was easy, he thought, for them to figure that it would be substantial, seeing Effy knew how much he was paid, and she knew close to how much he had spent while their relationship was ongoing. The fact that he showed her his money belt was enough for her to pass on that info to Effy who expected to seize quite a good amount. The "that's all" remark when he opened the money belt told Cane he was expecting a lot more. He nodded off to sleep as a slight smile broke across his face.

A heavy thud and engines firing into retro told him that had landed some three hours later at a small municipal airport just outside Bern. Fetching his duffle bag, which he had placed in the overhead bin just above him, he disembarked into a cold, drizzlely early morning in Bern. The terminal building was quiet and almost deserted, except for about three administrative staff, who probably knew about this flight coming. The passport officer did not even look up when he was presented Cane's British passport with a black man's picture as an English businessman. After all, most European countries were colonial rulers at some time, so, in Switzerland, nationalities are what their passport said they were. There was no luggage to claim, so Cane made his way to the exit. Many of the passengers had friends, relatives, or other arrangements waiting them. There was even a bus-type vehicle, which probably housed about forty persons, that was filled up quite quickly. Cane hesitated at the exit as he had no coat, and it was cold, wondering if he should put on another shirt and see if he could secure a taxi "out there somewhere" very quickly at this time of the morning. The one or two that were about was dispatched with a full load by other passengers before, and, Cane thought, possible arranged beforehand. No taxi operator was going just be waiting outside for a fare on the off chance that a passenger would need one this time of the morning. He ventured outside; it was cold, and he saw no semblance of anyone waiting to pick up a fare.

He reentered the building and tried to find a phone so he could call a taxi and saw Jacques lumbering towards the exit, trying to manipulate with three big duffel bags and a large suitcase. Cane hailed him and offered to help. Jacques welcomed the assistance, and in the exchange that followed, let Cane know that there was a car outside for him and he was going to Bern. He asked Cane to wait by the door with the luggage while he went for the car. Some time elapsed before the flashing of headlights at the door indicated to Cane that Jacques returned. As they loaded the luggage into the Citroen XLT, which resembled a throwback from World War Two, with his running boards, huge headlights, and very low total displacement to the ground. Once loaded, Cane marveled at the amount of space that was inside. Built for five comfortably, Cane figured it could easily hold ten.

As they drove, Jacques opened up in English, telling Cane that the car was placed at the airport for him by a younger brother who resided in Dieppe. Once the war was over, they had made contact and arrangements. Jacques had lost two friends during the war, one Swiss, Toussaint, and the other, Romano, Italian. They were ambushed while covering an RNA retreat, and it was so well executed that they lost about eighty percent of their unit fatally. Jacques suspected the ambush was arranged by Biafran European mercenaries. He was delivering the cremated remains of each to their families and other personal effects. Once that was over, he would be driving down to Milan and then onto Dieppe. His wife and two children still resided there. Jacques said he had fought in Nam and was wounded and sent back to France. After healing, he figured that the money the Biafrans were offering was worth another go at been a mercenary.

It was warm inside the car, and Cane found himself relating his experience of the war. He explained that he was actually sent by the British and was in fact an RNA soldier during the war on a soldier's pay. Dawn was breaking as they came to the outskirts of Bern. It was decided that they would split whatever expenses they incurred, and Jacques would drop him at the train station in Dieppe so he could catch transport to Calais, and from there, something to England.

The city was waking as Jacques maneuvered around the highways of Lake Geneva until they came to what Cane saw was a coffee shop that served a lot of breakfast items. Jacques parked and beckoned Cane to enter with him. A woman in about her early fifties, but looking strikingly attractive, looked towards the door as the bell chimed when they entered. She immediately flew from behind the counter straight to Jacques, and they embraced for a while. They were still in the embrace when a man, who could only be her husband, and from his Swiss exclamation, which Cane could not quite pick up, joined in the embrace. Cane was introduced, and they were ushered to a table slightly away from the others. Apparently, Cane surmised, this table was for special customers. Cane was famished, and all manner of breakfast savories started to arrive, with a steaming pot of coffee. This couple Jacques explained were Toussaint's parents and an only son. There were two other female siblings that lived elsewhere in Bern with their own families. After he was sated, Cane arose and headed towards the door. He was stopped by Mrs. Toussaint as she spoke to someone in Swiss, and shortly after, a man appeared with a coat and handed it to Cane. It was a perfect fit. Apparently, he was the same build as their son. He stepped outside and felt the clean, crisp, cold air engulf his body. He marveled at the cleanliness of the place as far as the eye could see. There was not a scrap of litter anywhere, not even a gum wrapper fluttering along. Earlier on, at the table, Jacques had excused himself, and with the father, had unloaded Toussaint's duffel bag from the car.

Jacques said that the drive to Milan would take about five hours, bypassing Zurich, and leaving now, they should be in Milan by midafternoon. Cane said his goodbyes in French, and they reciprocated, wishing him all the best for the future. Jacques said in French that he did not know that Cane spoke French, and Cane replied in French that he could get by. They both laughed as they got into the car.

For the next few hours, they exchanged chit chat about their families, work, achievements and hope for the future. Jacques said that this car was his father's who was a mechanic during the war, and when the Germans abandoned Paris after the war, he was able to get it. He had it purring like a well-fed cat in mouse hostel and still cautioned Jacques to take care of his baby whenever he used it. They were about two hours out of Milan when they stopped by a roadside cafe for lunch. As they sat chitchatting, Jacques said he thought it would be better for Cane to be dropped in Paris. He explained that there were better chances of finding out what his status was at the British Embassy and whatever was happening he would have more options rather than a small city like Dieppe. It was up to him. Cane mused over the idea for a few minutes and opted for Paris.

They arrived in Milan late afternoon, and Jacques headed for a cul de sac just off the San Siro Stadium. It was an apartment building, and Jacques led the way to the fifth floor. As the elevator doors opened, Cane helped Jacques lug the suitcase to an apartment door and rang the bell. A replay of what took place in Bern was reenacted, except that this was an apartment, not a coffee shop. There was mom, pop, teenage son and daughter. After the introductions and an invitation to dinner, Jacques agreed to stay the night, as there was so much they wanted to hear from him. The dinner consisted of spaghetti bolognaise with meatballs, garlic bread with lots of parmesan cheese, washed down with liters of red vino. After dinner, Cane was ready for a rest.

He and Jacques would share the guest room, and after breakfast tomorrow, they could be on their way. It was apparent that Jacques knew them before, and Cane made his way to the guest room as they continued to esquire about how, where, and what happened for their son to lose his life. Cane had showered and was adjusting his money belt when Jacques came into the room. Jacques smiled on seeing the belt and said jokingly, "That where you keep your Nigerian fortune?"

Cane told him, without saying how much, that it was taken from him at Ikeja by Effy and was left with only five hundred USD and few Nigerian dollars, which he had on him. Jacques remembered that Cane had asked him earlier about money seizure on the plane and said at least he left him some. They laughed. Seeing the ivory amulet with the unusual string around Cane's neck, Jacques enquired about it. Cane was glad to enlighten him about its acquisition.

Cane awoke about ten p.m. fully rested, and the apartment was quiet and dimly lit, with a few nightlights glowing in the passageway. There was sound in the kitchen, and Cane entered and saw Mr. Romano sipping some vino. Cane explained that he was rested and wanted to go for a little walk, and could he get a key so when he came back he would not disturb the household? He could not understand why Mr. Romano was looking at him, wide-eyed, with his mouth open while reaching into his pocket and handing him a key. As he turned away, he heard him say, "Mama mia, a black man speaking fluent Italian."

Cane smiled as he exited the door.

Outside, the night was cool, and as he left the cu de sac and reached the main street, the dazzle of neon advertising everything from cars, scooters to pizza was dazzling.

There were quite a few sidewalk pizzerias, which offered all the traditional Italian cuisine. One sign caught his eye, and he shook his head. Coca-Cola was offered at one hundred liras per liter bottle, while several named vinos were offered at twenty liras per liter bottle. Just as he rounded a block corner, he froze. Emanating from down the block was the unmistakable faint sound of Jamaican blue beat rhythms. It was Millie Small singing "My Boy Lollipop," which was a hit in Britain a few years back. Like the rats in the Pied Piper, Cane followed to the source of the sound. In doing so, he passed a line of about forty to fifty persons in their early to mid-twenties who were lining up to go into a club that had a sign in bold flashing neon, which read, "AYAITDEY."

Cane smiled. That was no language, it was plain Jamaican patois, which translated to "it is here." The record ended, and another took it place. Cane recognized it to be Owen Grey's "Please Let Me Go." Cane was confused. What was a Jamaican club doing in Milan, Italy, playing blue beat, and who was operating it? He had worked his way up to the entrance, which was blocked by a bouncer-type examining something each patron showed him before letting them him. He looked up and saw Cane, and for whatever reason beckoned for him to enter. Inside the club was noisy, dimly lit, with a huge ball turning in the ceiling, diffusing different lights, which varied in color and tensity. From the look on faces of the patrons, they were enjoying themselves, gyrating to the music in any fashion that suited the individual. There was no uniformity of movements. Cane wandered to a second-tier platform where the deejay was doing his thing, and as he saw Cane, without breaking his stride, he indicated to Cane with head movements to an reflective glass office on another upper tier. The sign on the door said, "PRIVATE," and Cane knocked.

"Yes," the voice inside said. "Come in." He did. And came face to face with a man in his late twenties or early thirties who, by complexion and hair, was a product of a mix union.

Cane said, "Are you the owner or boss?

He did not answer immediately, and his answer was "You are a Jamaican." Cane nodded, and the man introduced himself as Gary Parson, originally from Jamaica and London, and now Milan.

Cane sipped several merlots as Gary enthusiastically filled him in on AYAITDEY. He was born in Milan early in the war to an Italian mother and Jamaican father. After the war ended, his parents were facing a lot of hostility from the locals and made a decision.

His parents moved to London, as his mom's parents were not too keen on the idea of their daughter marrying a black man. There were hundreds of black men in Italy at that time, and quite a few of them intermarry. His father was in the Royal Air Force as a radar operator and decided they would be better off in England. Prejudice was everywhere, but with the influx of Commonwealth black men in England, he figured it would be better for the family. He was sent to Jamaica almost every holiday, and on a few occasions, his mom and dad, a younger sister and brother would also go and visit his grandparents. On his finishing school, he did not want to go to college and preferred traveling all over Europe. He was very surprised when he was told that his mother's parents wanted see him. He visited them, and never left Milan. He had found his niche. He went into the club business with the help of his Italian grandfather after he noted that all the clubs offered the same thing with hardly any differentiation between. He decided to be different three years ago and never looked back. From time to time, he would be interrupted by staff members about something pertaining to the club or clients, which he handled and quickly returned to his story while refilling Cane's glass with a high-quality merlot. He said, "Cane, easy access to me means my staff assumed that because you are black, you must have business with me." Cane realized that he could hear no music while in the office, and it was only when a staff member entered, he could hear briefly before the door closed. The office, although not large, had sofas and ottomans, tables and shelves, with a mini wet bar in one corner. His desk was mainly thick glass, with four matching sets of chairs. Gary pointed to a door, through which he said was his apartment. Cane glanced around at the numerous pictures hung on the wall with Gary and obvious celebrities, some old, some young. However, he wondered why such a successful, handsome young man was not married or why none of the pictures depicted him in close embrace with any of the few female pictures. He also became aware that every occasion that Gary would touch him, he would let his hands linger before removing them from that part where he rested it.

Cane was not a drinker and refused the last refill about two a.m., saying he had to return to the apartment with his friend. Gary said he was welcome to stay, "my casa es su casa," and showed some annoyance when Cane insisted that he had to leave. Cane went into the bathroom to refresh himself and noticed there were not anything female inside the whole apartment. He had expected to see something female to indicate that Gary shared it with someone, and since he did not say anything regarding that aspect of his life, plus the stay over invitation, Cane decided he would not mention anything. Gary said that he operates on Fridays and Saturdays from nine p.m. to four p.m. and during the week from nine p.m. to two p.m. Closing on Mondays. As Cane exited the bathroom, he felt giddy and almost fell as Gary caught him and nestled him on the nearby sofa. Cane awoke, still feeling a bit woozy, and saw on the wall clock; it was just before five a.m. Just then, Gary entered the office in a dressing gown and gushed all over Cane that he would have been more comfortable if he had indeed stayed in a comfortable bed, but he was glad to see him awake. Cane could not help but feel that something was wrong. They shook hands with the promise that if he was ever in Milan he would visit, and stepped out of the office. The ceiling disc was still turning slowly, but the crowd had gone, and it appeared as if the "night workers" were cleaning up. Exiting the club, he noticed the street was nearly deserted, and he made his way quickly to the cul de sac apartment. Letting himself in, he could hear Jacques's snoring, and as be began to undress, he was surprised to find that his pants zipper was down and the front of his underwire felt slightly damp. A weird thought entered his mind, but he quickly dismissed it as he flopped down on the bed and fell sleep almost as soon as he hit it.

Awaking a few hours later, he looked over and saw that Jacques's bed was empty and the morning light was creeping in through the window. As he showered, the last thought of the night crept back into his mind . He knew that Gary was definitely gay and wondered how far he had gone while he was out, obviously drugged. He smiled as he checked his body and concluded that only a frontal assault may have happened, but since he did not willingly participate, he hoped Gary, if he did, enjoyed himself. Dressing, he emerged into the kitchen and was quite surprised to see the whole family there, including Jacques, and in unison, they said good morning in Italian. Cane smiled and sat on an indicated seat by Papa who had informed everyone that he spoke Italian. Over breakfast, Jacques explained that they would be here for one more night as he would be running an errand with Papa and probably would not be back until late. Alphonso interrupted and asked about his club experience with a slight grin on his face. He said he sneaked in once and really loved the set up. Continuing, he said plain clothes detectives from time to time would pop in and run routine checks to see if anyone was using drugs, but so far he had never heard that anyone was caught using. Papa said he bet they did because rich people, after a while, they get bored and want to experiment. There was no consensus after Papa spoke, and Jacques, continuing, said they could leave then or the next morning. Since Jacques did not expand on the errand he was running nor invited him, Cane said okay to what was outlined.

He was back in the room, watching TV when he saw that Inter Milan would be playing Real Madrid in a crucial encounter between the two at the San Siro Stadium this Saturday afternoon at four p.m. Cane called Alphonso, the younger son, and inquired how could he get tickets for the match. Alphonso informed that regular tickets were sold out days ago, but he could get scalper ticket for the equivalent of thirty USD. With nothing to do until Jacques returned, he gave Al forty dollars. Cane loved soccer, and while he was in England was a fan of Tottenham Hotspur and also Manchester United. Al returned a short while later with a grandstand ticket and informed him he should line up about three-thirty p.m. to make sure he got in on time.

As the line moved towards the turnstile, with each person with ticket in hand, Cane glanced further down and saw several huge stacks of cushions, which were depleting quickly as he gazed. Apparently, they were sold to patrons as they entered. Seating in a comfortable armchair-type seat, Cane looked around the huge stadium. The playing field was completely separated from the all the stands with very tall wire fences. The crowd around him was a mixture of both teams' fans from their chatter of support as to who would win.

The ohs, ahs, short-lived chorus of goal, as that particular kick was saved, echoed continuously as the two teams fought for supremacy. Finally, as the final whistle blew, both teams were locked in a two-two all tie. The whistle brought an avalanche of cushions thrown over the fences. Apparently, all seats except for the grandstand were just concrete tiers, hence the cushions to soften the hiney. Returning to the apartment, Al informed him that the cushion thing was a common feature at all matches. He was not certain if they were recycled after the stadium cleaners cleared the grounds.

Cane was anxious to be on the move, and when Jacques called to say that there would be an indefinite delay as to when he and Papa would return, his spirits fell.

Mrs. Ramona saw the look on his face when he came to dinner and somehow empathized with him. "You know you are welcome to stay here as long as you wait for Jacques," she ventured. "If you want to go, there is a train from Milano Porta Garbibaldi that leaves just after midnight for Lyon in France." Cane smiled and thank her. A taxi to the train station was about thirty minutes, and after some more chit chat, Cane retired to his room.

At eleven p.m., the taxi that was called arrived, and Cane said his goodbyes and departed. He was sorry that he had missed seeing Jacques, but as the taxi pulled into the train station, he knew that this was another chapter in his life that was now closed. Cane bought a single private sleeper berth and settled in. The dining car did not close until three a.m., so, before tucking in, he had a light supper in the almost empty dining car.

It was about seven-thirty a.m. when Cane awoke feeling quite rested and clear headed. The train was about an hour from Lyon, and he could smell the strong odor of coffee wafting through the train. He dressed and entered a now-crowded dining car where all tables were taken and was shown a table with a young very blond man sitting alone. After placing his breakfast order, the young man introduced himself in French as Wolfgang Muller, an engineer who was on his way to take up a job at the Citroen car factory. Cane replied who he was in French.

Other pleasantries were exchanged as they ate breakfast. As the train whistled, huffed, and puffed and acres of rolling fields whisked past, Cane could see workers in vineyards and fields. It came as quite a surprise to him when Wolfgang said with disdain, "Look at them, look at those peasants, and yet they won the war." He had spoken in German, not knowing that Cane would understand.

Pretending, Cane asked what he said, and he replied for Cane to forget it. Excusing himself, Cane went back to his berth and contemplated what would he be doing in Paris on a Sunday morning.

Paris was chilly, but he had the coat from Bern. Exiting the station, he saw Paris just coming awake, and a Champs Elysee that was not bustling. The Eiffel Tower was off in the distance. Not knowing where to pass the time, he entered the first open cafe he saw. A waiter approached. "*Parley vous francais monsieur la homme noir?*"

Cane smiled and replied in French that he did and placed his order for the breakfast special that was advertised on a large menu at the entrance. He smiled to himself after the waiter left because to be called a black man without any disparaging connotations is very rare. It was quite appropriate, Cane thought, since he did not know him, although there were black Frenchmen from the French African colonies. After breakfast, Cane took a taxi to the Eiffel Tower. It was still mid-morning, and he would visit Paris like a tourist for a while, then get a train to Calais or a ferry to whichever English port, and finally, a train to London. It did not make sense to him at this stage to overnight in Paris, at God knows nowhere, and visit the UK Embassy when he could do the real thing in London. He knew London, not Paris. He stopped at a roadside café and began to study a map he had bought. He did not want to be changing his mode of transport more than once because he knew each time he did, he would have to produce his passport or some form of identification, and only God knew what Sir Robert had set up if he tried to enter England.

By the time he had visited and climbed the stairs at the Eiffel Tower, take in the grandeur of the Arc de Trompe, he figured it was time to get a train. He found one leaving Gare Du Nord in about an hour directly to Calais to link up with a ferry to Folkstone and a train to Victoria, London. There would be only one passport examination to board at Calais.

The crowd had grown, and as he made his way down, he was constantly bumped and pushed by those going up. Finally, at the bottom of the tower, he sat down and ordered a liter of merlot and began to sip as he went through his personal things in his bag and check his finances. Suddenly, he realized that his heartbeat had increased unnaturally, and he was breathing in short gaps. While going over his things in his bag, he did not see his passport, which was always in the inside pocket. He now began to search frantically, emptying out everything on the table and floor. Curious passersby were commenting about the black man going loco. Having exhausted every nook and cranny of his bag, he concluded that he did not have it; he even patted himself down. He did not need it when he boarded the train in Milan, and the last time he saw it was when he packed his things at the apartment. He still had on his coat, and he remembered putting the map in the inside pocket and was sure he felt the passport then. Could he have been picked when he was jostled descending? All sorts of wild ideas came rushing in his brain, even that he was recognized by some agent of Sir Robert who ordered his passport lifted by any means. His mood was dark; despair had set in; so near and yet so far. His laminations became audible, and he took some deep breaths and decided to analyze his situation and work out a solution. He stopped short, hurried into the café, and obtained some francs and found a phone booth. His French got him through to the operator in Milan, and his Italian got him through to Mrs. Romano and the apartment. Mrs. Romano was not surprised to hear from him as before he could say anything, she told him that she had found his passport on the dresser in the guest room. He was speechless and finally thanked her, asking that she express post it to the address he gave her. He would send her whatever it cost as soon as he got it. He had figured that Milan was one place he could have left it and had asked the café owner if he found, it could he have it sent to this address. While contemplating, Cane placed a hundred francs into his hand and *oui oui* came very quickly.

The passport would take between two to three days to get here, and so Cane knew that he had to find somewhere to stay until its arrival. He knew that around this area hotels and other places of abode would be expensive, so he had to find other areas that he could afford. He still had the map and was studying it again when he heard above the usual din of traffic and people.

"God, I am bored in this place."

The accent was definitely American, female, and southern. He glanced around from the where the voice came from and immediately recognized the redhead sitting by herself as the person who uttered the phrase. She was in her late forties or earl fifties, tanned, well dressed, and sported an engagement and wedding ring on the appropriate finger. All in all, although no ravishing beauty, she was an attractive mature woman.

Cane wandered where her other half was and noticed only one chair was pulled out from the table, and he was either late in coming or she was on her own. Just having come out of minor depression, he decided that he would try to make her acquaintance and see where it leads. He went over and asked in French if he may join her.

Looking up, she could not believe that a black man was saying something to her and began to shake her head negatively. She was not saying no he can't join her, she was saying that she did not understand. She finally got out "no understand," and Cane repeated in American drawl. She burst out laughing and invited him to be seated.

She was still laughing mildly, and Cane noticed the wine she was drinking and ordered two more in French from the waiter who appeared at the table. The questions came out in a tumble, who are you, where are you from, what are doing here, etc. Cane halted her and told her a little about himself and the purpose of his presence. She was taken aback. She confirmed that she was Alabama in the USA and was on her way to Brussels to set up home for her diplomatic husband who has just be named Under Secretary of Trade to the EEC. She had stopped in Paris to see her daughter who was doing her doctorate in International Politics at the Sorbonne.

They continued exchanging tidbits about their lives as they sipped wine, and Cane realized that they had not eaten. He ordered dinner as close to an American meal that was on the menu and continued exchanging tidbits. Time passed, and it then dawned on Cane that he had not found anywhere to stay until his passport arrived. He relayed this information to her and made his excuse to leave. As he was getting up, she mentioned for him to remain seated.

"Please do not take this as an invitation for anything than me just giving an helping hand." Cane was puzzled. "I am staying at the Elyees Chateu, a hotel about ten minutes from here. My daughter was supposed to stay with me for a few more days, but after two days she left, and I have a whole suite to myself. You are welcome to stay, as there is a huge sofa bed in the front room." Cane never looked a gift horse in the mouth, and if this was a genuine no obligation offer, he was okay with it. She said the hotel was booked in her name with a guest, so there would be no problem.

They decided to walk after Cane paid the bill and reminded the owner about the incoming post. As they walked, they continued talking about nothing and everything. She said she had chosen Spanish as her second language as she had hoped her that he diplomatic husband's career was heading to Spain. She had married right after completing her degree in Political Science and was Mrs. Betty Mae Malia Wilkins of the Alabama. Her husband family had money and clout, and her marriage to young Wilkins starting his diplomatic career was hailed far and wide in Alabama. She was crowned Miss Alabama the year before, making the union even more newsworthy. Her maiden name was Hasley, and they, too, were a family that was not poor, although not as rich as the Wilkins. They were walking at a slow, leisurely pace, when Cane stopped, and when a broad grin appeared on his face, she was puzzled.

The grin became a broad smile, and Cane said finally, "BMW, that is the name of a car."

She did not get it at first, then she also smiled and said, "Top of the line." She later confined that she had never been in close proximity to a black man. Yes, many black men were in Alabama, but socially, she had never had to occasion to mix. She wondered if she was in her hometown, would she be walking down the street in broad daylight, chatting away to a black man? More than likely, if that happened, she was sure that later that night some men in hooded white robes would pay him a visit.

Reaching the hotel, they went straight to the lift and ascended to the fifth floor. Her suite was a one bedroom, with a den and siting room. There was indeed a huge sofa bed there. Pillows, blankets, and a sheet were placed for him, and she said she would use to bathroom first and then he would be free to do so. After hearing her humming in the bathroom for some time and then silence, Cane decide to have a bath. He had heard about continental bathrooms, but he was still surprised when he opened the door. Instead of as flat tub, it was tubular, and once you closed the door and turned on the water, it filled up from ankle up. Cane took his shower and returned to his sofa bed, turned on the TV, and decided to relax for the rest of the evening.

The phone rang a couple of times in the next hour and was answered in the bedroom. Cane was just about dozing when Betty Mae came out of her bedroom in nightgown and dressing gown covering her entire body like a cocoon. She was brushing her long red hair and sat on the far side of the sofa as she continued doing so. Cane turned off the TV as she had said something to him, but he did not hear and ask her to repeat. "Tell me about Jamaica," she said as she continued to brush her hair. Cane was glad to expose about his homeland and left out nothing to the point he got to Sandhurst. She was intrigued has to how he became so fluent in languages. Finally, Cane asked her to expand on some of the things she had already told him, and when she finished, he realized that with the makeup off, she was still an attractive woman. The conversation had veered a little when she told him that as a diplomat wife, it was boring because after you attended some many Embassy parties, it was no longer something you look forward to. Plus, after each party, one would arrive home tired or tipsy, and sex would go out of the window. She was glad she had her kids early in the marriage, as sex became less and less as they grew older. Her son was a breech birth, and once they cut her, she had her tubes tied. That birth also put an end to her bikini-wearing at the beach as the scar was too visible.

At this point, Cane could not help but ask her about her sex life as it seemed her husband had lost interest and what was the reason for it. She said that she did not think he had a mistress or anything like that as, from time to time, he would reach for her, especially on a weekend, and they would make love, but that was happening less and less, and she hoped his move to Brussels would give him more time for her, but she doubted it. Her daughter, who was always close to her dad, suddenly said she wanted to go abroad to study after finishing high school, and she was sent to one of the best universities in Switzerland. Her son finished at Yale and was now going to Columbia Law School. Cane sensed that there was more to it than what she was saying about her husband and daughter's relationship but did not pursue it.

The doorbell rang, and she got up and went to door. After a moment or two and a brief exchange, she returned with a tray with several club sandwiches, ice, and two bottles of vino. Before she had come out, she had ordered the tray to be sent up in about an hour. She had done this on two previous occasions when her daughter was there, only that both of them were in the bedroom. After finishing wining and dining, she left for the bathroom and returned to say goodnight. Cane noticed that her robe was loose as she approached the sofa, and he could now make out her upturned, pert breast through the see-through nightie.

She bent over to kiss him on his cheek and let the kiss linger for a while as Cane turned slightly and found her lips closing in on his. Her perfume was strong but sensual, and Cane could not control the rise of his manhood. She was on top of him, and he felt her ushering his manhood into her as she moaned slightly. He was fully committed to making love to her, and she moaned and gasped each time he thrust into her as he was now on top. Cane wanted the release as well and so moved more rapidly until just as he was about to come and heard her moan loudly, and she dug her hands into his back as her body went limp. He was totally exhausted as he rolled off, and she was moaning softly as she lay there.

Looking at her well-toned and tanned body, pert breasts, still firm even after having two kids, he wondered how a man could not want to be having her every chance he got. She was sleeping now, and he lifted her up and took her into the bedroom and covered her with the spread and returned to his sofa.

He had no expectation of what the day would bring, but he hoped she would not be remorseful or angry about the events the night before. She was an American Southerner woman who saw black men as a reality that she had to live with but not a part of her daily life. His concerns were shattered as her bedroom flew open and she was on him before he could even rise to the occasion. But as she touched him, he did, and the episode of night was repeated. It was about eight a.m. when they came up for air and were still locked in an embrace. Their lovemaking had lasted pretty close to an hour.

"Cane," she began, "when I awoke I could not believe what had happened, but as I got more to thinking about it, I found myself wanting you more and more and my body warming, so I said, 'in for a penny in for a pound,' and here I am."

Cane laughed quietly and said he had vision of her screaming, "Rape, rape!" and French *gerdames* would come busting down the door and haul him off to jail. She began to laugh so much that tears stream down her face.

She said, still laughing, that scenario was not as farfetched as he imagined because she was sure that many white women in the South had freely given themselves to a black, only to scream rape when it was over and reality hit them as to what they had to face forever from that day.

As they prepared for the day, she said that she had ordered breakfast of French toast, bacon, sausage, regular toast, coffee, and orange juice. After breakfast Betty Mae suggested that she would really appreciate if he would accompany her to the Moulin Rouge nightclub, as there was no way she was going to visit Paris and not go there. She had asked to hotel clerk to make the reservations for her and her daughter, which he did, but her daughter had left. He could get evening clothes to rent at the hotel boutique since the club is formalwear and he may not have in his bag.

"Listen, I don't want you to feel any obligation, as I know you will be leaving as soon as your passport is obtained, so don't do anything I suggest if you don't want to."

Cane said he was okay with everything so far and told her if she is ever in Milan she should visit the AYAITDEY club. It would be a different experience.

Cane took one last look in the mirror as she ushered out of the apartment, and was pleased with what he saw. Her dress, too, was revealing enough without been vulgar. Unlike the time when he was in a cab with Jennifer and the driver maintained a disgusting look, this one was complimenting them as a couple as soon as we gave him his destination. Betty Mae had slipped a bundle of cash into his hands along with the tickets for the club as they entered the cab. On arrival, he gave the driver one of the notes and the gushing "Merci, merci" indicated that it was more than enough. The tickets were for a VIP entrance, and Cane was, what can only be described as struck with awe, at the majestic decor of the place as they were taken to their reserved table. He had heard of the club in glorious tones from time to time, and it certainly lived up to the hype. Returning to the hotel, both were tipsy, and the lovemaking that followed confirmed that the champagne at the club had reduced their resistance to hold back any of their feelings. They both fell into a long and deep slumber.

Counting today and possible two more days (that's three nights), both of them would be leaving to go their separate ways. Cane could not help thinking that if it played out that way, it would be another closed chapter in his life. And it did. After two days, he received his passport, and the last three nights were spent in wanton abandon and Betty Mae let the shackles of all her inhibitions loose even more so and enjoyed the full intimacy of lovemaking. As they parted, she to the airport and him to the train station, there was moment of silence as they searched for words to express what happened over the last few days. In the end, they just embraced, and she was gone.

It was only two and a half hours to Calais, and before he knew it, he was disembarking at Folkstone. There were a large group of people with British passports in hand entering a line so designated, and Cane saw that the officer at the desk barely glanced at them. The officer did hesitate for a second as he gave Cane the once over, comparing the picture and person standing before him. A black man with an English passport was not unusual, as just yesterday four Chinese men from Hong Kong passed through with British passports. Cane was lucky; had the officer took time to really read the passport, the outcome might have been different as Cane passport's number was on a restricted list that laid on the counter.

The train ride from Folkstone to Kings Cross Station was uneventful. He had found a solo seat, and since it was non-stop to London, no one came to join him. London was chilly as well, and for a few moments, as Cane joined the taxi line outside the station, he could not believe that it was over three years ago he had left England and he was back on English soil. The line moved quickly, and he gave his old address to the driver. As he said it, his heart began to beat faster in anticipation of seeing his wife. London had not changed much. As the cab weaved its way through the traffic, he noted new buildings going up here and there. The cab swung down Hyde Park Corner, and Cane gasped. He was not aware that he was passing Speakers Corner. The significance of Sunday evening in London had slipped him. This was where his troubles, so to speak, first started. A large crowd was gathered at a particular speaker's podium, and Cane wandered what his oratory was about.

The taxi pulled up in front of the building, and Cane noted that there were a few structural changes and fresh paint. After paying the driver, he half expected to see the curtains move at "his" apartment, but nothing happened, so he rang the bell to flat one. He did not recognize the voice that said, "Yes, can I help you?" Taken aback, he did not answer immediately. The person repeated the question again.

"Can I speak to Mercedes?" he finally blurted out.

"Who?" the voice said.

Cane repeated, growing even more anxious.

"I am sorry, you have the wrong flat. There is no Mercedes living here," said the voice and ended the call. Frustration built up in Cane. He wanted to see a person, explain that that was his and Mercedes' flat, and find out where she had gone. He even looked at the numbered buzzers again to make sure that he had rung the right one. Standing there seething was not an option. He walked to the corner, hailed a cab, and told the driver to take him to a hotel in the Fulham Road, which he knew. He told the receptionist a week instead of just for a night as the weekly rate was considerably less. Not that cost was a problem, as he had not even gone into his secret compartment in his duffle bag.

Cane went over to a pub called the Golden Swan and ordered fish and chips and a large lager. The fish and chips tasted as only the English can make it, and he ordered another. As he ate and sipped, he began to plan what his movements would be tomorrow. He made a mental list and wrote it down when he returned to the hotel before going to sleep.

The next morning, after a typical English breakfast consisting of eggs, bacon, sausage, and toast at the hotel, he felt energized, calm, and ready to take on the world.

Most businesses opened at nine a.m., so he ate leisurely, biding his time for his first call. It was at the Weatherly rental office. The mixed-race young man who greeted him could be no other than Mr. Weatherly's son. The resemblance was so striking. Cane introduced himself, related his first encounter with his dad, he had presumed correctly, his absence, without telling him why, and his seeking info as to where the previous tenants were. Young Weatherly told him that his parents had sold several of their properties and retired to Belize. In turn, they had bought up quite a number of more modern apartment buildings, and he, his brother, and sister ran the business from this office. His sister did the bookwork, his brother the day-to-day management, and he the clerical. He had no files after the property was sold about two years ago. Accepting his apology that there was nothing further he could do, Cane took his leave. The next point of call was the British Home Office building. His visit here was twofold: he wanted to find out about his passport, and also how could he get in touch with Sir Robert Morley at MI5.

Inside the huge auditorium, there were signs and directions all over the place, along with uniformed customer service reps as well. Receptionists had huge letterings above them from A to Z. Cane met a smiling attractive female customer service rep. He told her his passport was valid, but he needed to see someone about it as he thought it was restricted. She took the passport from him, leafed through it, and nodded for him to follow her. She went to a nearby phone, and Cane watched her as she spoke, nodded, spoke, nodded a few times, then hung up. She pinned a tag on him, told him to discard it in the box at the door when leaving, and was directed to an office number on the fourth floor. Handing him his passport, she smiled and left to another customer.

Cane was passing a public pay phone when he decided to a call a particular number.

Anyone observing him would have thought he had gone nuts as he burst out laughing quite audible as he left the phone kiosk. The answer he got when he called the number from Lagos was the same he was getting now. His laughter had attracted one or two customer reps who moved towards him. On seeing his tag, they indicated the direction he should take and went back to other customers.

Arriving at the designated office, Cane knocked and entered on the "Come in."

The voice belonged to a man in his late fifties who, without introducing himself, asked Cane for the passport and his reason for his visit. After hearing Cane's story about the non-priority in his attempt to leave Lagos and return to England, the man left through a rear door. The office was bland, metal desk, typewriter, and a few chairs and what appeared to be a few personal items on the desk.

About twenty minutes later, the man returned with a file, and after scanning what appeared to be papers, Cane was trying to see it because he could read upside down, but the file was placed too far from him on the desk.

He spoke. "Mr. Cane, here is your passport; the restriction is lifted. Further than that, I cannot say more. Your request to get an appointment with Sir Robert Morley will be passed on, and if you leave an address or phone number with receptionist D in the foyer, you will be contacted. Good day to you, sir." Cane left the building and stepped out into hustle and bustle of a London street in the West End. Earlier on, he had made an appointment to have dinner at the upscale Chinese restaurant, "The Yantengse River" in Earls Court, which was reputed to be one of the best in London.

He had always had a love for authentic Chinese food and had decided that as soon as he was able in terms of time, he would indulge himself. His dinner date was five p.m., and looking at his watch, he had about two hours to kill before his appointment.

Cane decided to take the "underground," as that form of train transport was called, to his dinner date.

The subway station was not crowed, and in no time a train heading for Earls Court pulled in. He saw a four-seat empty space with each two-seater facing each other and took one. Glancing up at the information panel above each window showed the route the train took. Cane saw that he was four stations from where he should alight. The "mind the doors, please" and the "swoosh" closing of the doors and he was on his way. Just then, as the train started, a man took the seat opposite to him. As the train picked up, speed Cane closed his eyes and rested his head on the seat cushion above him. He had not taken any interest in the passenger in front of him, only that he was middle aged and white, but came out of his mild slumber when he felt a pressure on his legs. He opened his eyes quickly to stare into a broad grin from the passenger in front of him. At the same time, he wondered what the pressure on his leg was, and found that the man had placed his legs between Cane's and was squeezing them. Before he could say anything, the man, seeing that Cane was now aware of the situation, said, "Hi, lofty. I have got a lovely flat in Turnham Green that you would be happy sharing with me."

It took some time for the whole situation to sink in as to what was happening. Lofty was a term used by many of the working class to denote a tall person, so Cane realized that the man was focused on him. Cane glanced up on the travel map over the window and found that Turnham Green was some eight stations from this point. Cane smiled to himself as he found the situation very funny; here was a white man picking up a black man. The train had slowed considerably as it pulled into the next station, and a few passengers got up ready to disembark. Cane also got up, but instead of disembarking, took a seat at another empty space. To his dismay the man also followed. As the train pulled out of the station, the man again placed his legs between Cane's, and smiling, said, "Come on, sunshine, you will love it."

The coach had about ten to twelve passengers, and Cane realized that nobody had taken any interest in what was going on. Sunshine was a term the working classes used to be polite to a black person. Cane was wondering what his next move should be, when the man reached over and grabbed to front of Cane's pants, searching for his genitals. Cane grabbed his hand, bending back the thumb until the man was screaming in agony and at the same time slapping him across his face with the other. The man slid to the floor after the slap, and Cane could hear a chorus of screaming engulfing the carriage. The train was slowing down, indicating that it was approaching the next station. The man was still on the floor as the train stopped in the station and the doors were opened. Women passengers alighting were screaming and the men hurrying. Cane had no idea how far underground was this station, but he saw several policemen entering the carriage, and before he could say anything, his hands were behind him, and he heard the click of handcuffs closing. The escalator was two stories down, and as he and the two police escorts reached the street level, a police car pulled up, and he was hustled into it. Up to this point, no one or anything was said to him.

Arriving at the police station, he was escorted into a room with several benches and told to sit. After about ten minutes of sitting, a policemen came and removed the handcuffs, which was a relief, as his shoulders had begun to ache a little. A plastic bag was placed in front of him and was told to put everything on his person into it. Looking around, Cane around saw a white man and black man, both of them looking very distressed, were his companions in the room. The memory of a previous sojourn in a police station flooded Cane's mind, and he shook his head as if to say "No, no, not again."

Just as he dozing, off a policemen came and indicated to him to follow him. Cane ended up in front of another policeman behind a huge circular desk.

"I am Sargent Bellows," the officer behind the desk said, "and you, Mr. Cane, are charged with assault and battery on one Mr. Martin Sealy. There are some papers in front of you, which you may sign as guilty as charged or not guilty. If you sign guilty as charged, then you will appear before a magistrate for sentencing tomorrow with no bail here; not guilty, then you are entitled to bail and you can choose either a jury or magistrate for trial and be defended by a lawyer. The trial date will be approximately two weeks hence."

Cane could not believe what he was hearing. A man on a train had sexually assaulted him, he had defended himself, and he was charged for that defense with the possibility of going to prison, according to Sgt. Bellows. Since he had no permanent address, he had to check it at this particular police station between six a.m. and six p.m. every day until the case is resolved. As soon as Cane left the station, he called the Yantegse Restaurant and apologized for not keeping the dinner date.

For the next two weeks, Cane dutifully reported to the police station after breakfast at the hotel each day. Initially, he had made a list of lawyers who took on cases such as his, but after the first two days of enquiry decided that he would never get one to represent him in court. The nonrepresentation followed a particular pattern. On the telephone, there was no way that the particular lawyer could distinguish that this potential client was not a socially acceptable Englishman. However, once the case was outlined and Cane told them that he was black, silence and date mix ups, and a lawyer would not be able became the routine to his enquiry, so Cane stopped. He decided that when the case came up, he would defend himself before a magistrate rather than a jury. This decision followed his getting a court date and the charges Mr. Sealy had laid against him. He figured that based on the simplicity of the events, it would be better for a magistrate to hear and decide rather than a jury. Several pairs of eyes looking at a black man and making a decision based on facts was too risky, Cane thought. One pair of eyes was a better risk. On his tenth reporting day, Sgt. Bellows gave him a brown envelope which consisted of papers he should hand to his lawyer, place of the trial, his court date (which was in ten days' time), papers seeking legal aid, and other legal steps to be taken before appearing. It was not every occasion when Cane went to the station he saw Sgt. Bellows, but the few times he did, they would have a little chit chat about the case. When Cane told him that he was defending himself, he cautioned Cane to seek a postponement until he found a lawyer that would represent him. Sgt. Bellow informed him that his earlier encounter with the police years ago was on file, but the CROWN (prosecutor) could not use it to influence the verdict of the magistrate but could do so in sentencing. Mr. Sealy had a conviction of indecent exposure, but Cane could not use that fact in outlining anything as previous actions had nothing to do with the case in question. If he was found guilty by the magistrate, he faced anything between six months to three years in prison depending on how the magistrate saw how the injuries incapacitated Mr. Sealy. Cane said he had tried but felt he needed to get this case over with, no matter the outcome, so he could move on with his life.

The next few days flew by quickly, and Cane spent his time researching similar cases at the library while also trying to get some lead on his wife. He had found a case extremely similar to his, except it was two white men, and decided he would handle his case that way. The accuser had lost.

Cane arrived early at the Court and took his seat. The court was schedule to start at nine-thirty a.m., and quite a number of people had arrived by that time. Looking at the cases that were down to be heard, they ranged from domestic abuse, traffic offense, shoplifting, and assault and battery. Cane got a rude awakening when the first case was called up. A lady charged with shoplifting. She had a lawyer, but the Crown (Her Majesty's lawyer) would prosecute for the Crown. Cane had an idea based on his research it would be his word against Mr. Sealy's word, but the CROWN was Mr. Sealy's lawyer, so to speak.

Cane was quite calm when his name was called and he approached the magistrate (who was a woman). He was asked if he had legal representation and if he required one, and magistrate informed him if he understood that whatever the outcome of this case there would be no appeal. Cane answered negatively and yes.

"Very well, Mr. Jones, proceed."

"M'lord, this is a very simple case. Mr. Sealy, while sitting quietly at a window seat on the subway, Mr. Cane requested that he changed seats with him for whatever reason. Mr. Sealy refused and was assaulted most viciously by Mr. Cane. That's it, m'lord."

"Call your first witness, Mr. Jones," said the magistrate.

Sealy was called and sworn in. He gave his name, date of birth, address, and profession. He repeated what the Crown outlined, adding that Cane dislocated his thumb while forcing him out of his seat. He had never seen him before and had never spoken to him except telling Cane that he was never giving up his seat as he had fought in the war to defend his rights. Cane noticed that the Crown was not offering any medical evidence and felt that was in his favor if it came to sentencing. He felt that no matter what he said (he had no witness to call), he was going to be found guilty as charged, and he wondered what he could say to mitigate a harsh sentence.

Cane was lost in thought and did not hear the first time when the magistrate asked if he had any questions for Mr. Sealy. "No," he finally stammered on her second asking. Mr. Jones informed her that was the Crown's case

"Mr. Cane, do you have any witnesses to call to refute Mr. Sealy's claim of assault?" asked the magistrate.

"No ma'am, Your Honor, sorry, my lord," Cane replied meekly.

"Are you taking the stand in your own defense?" she continued. Cane decided that he might as well since he had nothing to lose at this stage. As he was being sworn in, he saw Sgt. Bellows at the front pew.

Cane told his story in the best queen's English expected from a non-English person. When he indicated that he had finished, Mr. Jones asked in a very contemptuous manner that what he just related to the court was a pack of lies made up to defuse from the vicious attack he perpetrated against Mr. Sealy. Cane's mind was too weary to respond; he could not believe that the "Mother Country" was about to send him to prison for defending himself. He knew that what happened years ago was justified, especially three against one, but now one-on-one and he knew the black man was going to lose.

Just then he saw Sgt. Bellows got up and ask to approach Mr. Jones and the magistrate. They huddled for a few minutes, and the magistrate asked that Mr. Sealy (who had gone outside) be recalled to the stand.

"Mr. Sealy, you are wandering why I recalled you, but it is of utmost importance that your answer is as you recollect. The question is, did you speak to Mr. Cane in anyway before he attacked you?"

"God's truth, my lord, no way. That darkie just attacked me."

"Then please explain to this court how did Mr. Cane know that you lived in Turnham Green?"

The blood drained out of Sealy's face, spittle appeared on his lips and the corners of his mouth; he started to gulp like a goldfish in a bowl.

"Mr. Cane, you are dismissed from all charges pertaining to this case;

you are free to go."

Cane did not understand just what happened, but he was not going to hang around to find out, and in his rush to exit, he nearly ran over Sgt. Bellows who was just outside the exit door.

"Whoa, whoa, hold, Cane. No one is after you."

Cane stopped, caught his breath, and asked, "What happened in there?"

"Turnham Green, matey. When he gave his address as Pope Road in Turnham Green, I wondered how you could have known that before, and on reading your first statement when you were brought to the station, you said he invited you to come and share a flat in Turnham Green, so he must have spoken to you before you slapped him, so I just drew the court's attention to that as a 'friend of the court.'"

Cane was at a loss for words, and as he stared at a white policemen who just helped a black man, Sgt. Bellows grinned and said, "Look, at the end of the war, a black soldier saved my life. I don't know what company or country he was from, but I would not be here today if he did not take out that German soldier. I was wounded, and he disappeared before I could even say thanks as we were under heavy fire. This is the first occasion that I was able to repay my debt to a black man and at least say thanks to the unknown soldier."

Cane shook his hand, and they departed. Cane stood there for a minute, wondering what to do, then he smiled, went into a phone booth, and when the line answered, he said, "I would like to make a dinner reservation."

Cane stopped at the bank next and was pleasantly surprised without much ado he obtained his balance. What surprised him was from the time he left, no monies were withdrawn, and the account had nearly seven thousand pounds in it. Cane was perplexed. What the hell took place after he left his beautiful, loving wife? He was not feeling very hopeful as he entered the Barbados Embassy, but foreign embassies usually knew where their nationals were, and Barbados had gotten Independence from Britain right after Jamaica, hence they had their own embassy. The lady whom he was directed listened attentively as he related his quest to find his wife. After he was finished, she pointed out that Braithwaite was not an uncommon name in Barbados, much as Jones would be in a Welsh town. However, since he attached Mercedes and the father's name of Joseph to the name, plus he was wealthy, she would make the necessary enquirers. Since he did not have a permanent phone number or address, he should call the office and leave one when he did.

Over the next few days, Cane found a one-bedroom flat in a high-end apartment block; here it was the color of your money that allowed you in, not your skin color. He bought some new clothes at fashionable London boutique and visited predominantly West Indian areas like Brixton, Stoke Wilmington, Tottenham, and Camberwell, casually asking around the Hi Streets if anyone knew Mercedes or her father in Barbados. All hopeful leads had ended with no fulfillment. Several times in Lagos he had tried to get a call to Jamaica, but never succeeded. Now that he was in London, he thought of calling his grandmother, who probably had given him up for dead. She might have been in contact with Mercedes, but decided against it.

Sitting at the Yantese River Chinese restaurant, having an evening meal, he contemplated his options. He figured he had two main ones and two minor ones. His main was to fly to Barbados himself and see what he could discover or hire a detective to do. Either of those was going to dip into his finances a great deal, and as he had not sought a job yet, he would have to balance his financial output. What he had extracted from his duffle bag and lodged to his account would keep him stable for some time. He had also visited the WISC, and apart from the barman, no one knew him. As students qualified in their respective field, they would head home to their countries. In three years, the turnover of students was dramatic, and very few new students were coming from the Caribbean to England to study. The warden and his family had also moved on according to the barman to a cottage in Essex.

The Yantese River Chinese restaurant was in a very upscale area of Earls Court and patronize by the rich and powerful. Although neither, Cane was dressed to give that impression and felt for a good authentic Chinese meal; so, earlier on, he had made a reservation. He was seated to the rear, facing the door, and was about to put some food in his mouth, when in doing so he caught a glimpse of a couple entering and froze.

The infinite number of circumstances that welds together to make an event happen at a precise time for an individual are insurmountable. There are some many variables, so many transient things that could randomly happen to cause a detail to upend. Instead of looking up, had he looked down he would have missed the entrance, Sir Alec Softe, the minister of Trade and Industry in the present Conservative government, was removing Jennifer Keller's coat and handing it to the maitre'd. He was in the darker light where he sat, and she was in the brighter. In three years, she had become even more beautiful, attractive, gorgeous, he was running out of superlatives, to describe her. Still halfway up to his mouth with the food, he watched as they were escorted to a private booth and a nylon curtain drawn. The rich and powerful liked their privacy. Sir Softe, although about twenty years her senior, was known as a man about town and a bachelor. Cane reckoned that most complete meals took about an hour and a half to two hours, so he continued his meal leisurely and kept his eye on their booth.

It was nearly two hours before he saw them emerge and had an extra dessert to avoid just sitting there. He followed a few minutes after, leaving a generous tip, and went out with his head turned down in case she was looking that way. He saw the minister security personnel signaled for his car and went about three cabs down the taxi rank, that is always on hand for patrons, and watched. Other patrons were coming out as well, and as the connoisseur signaled for a cab, he hopped into the one he was standing beside. The cab driver was about to say something as Cane put a five-pound note in his hand. Cane said that he was a magazine reporter and wanted him to follow the minister's car to see if he was up to any hanky panky. The driver must have been anti-Conservative, as he smiled as the minister car pulled out into the traffic. Cane expected the cab to pull out almost at the same time but had to allow the minister security personnel car to do so first.

The traffic was not heavy, and the cab driver kept a safe distance behind the two cars, changing lanes often when they were on a long stretch. It would be impossible for any of the security to ascertain that a cab was following as there was so many different lookalike cabs busy prowling the London streets. They were all black and the same model. They arrived at Carlton Towers, a modern upscale thirty-story apartment building, about twenty20 minutes later. It was the dwelling place of the movers and shakers in

London and had the latest in high-tech security measures for his patrons. Among the many dwellers were politicians of both parties that had country houses in their consistencies but stayed in London during Parliamentary sessions. Cane had alighted from his cab down the block as soon as he saw their quarry had stopped, crossed the road into the shadows as his cab passed the ministers further down. The five pounds was more than enough.

Cane watched as Jennifer exited from the car and blew a kiss to Sir Softe. The two cars sped off, and she ascended the stairs to the Towers, but veered to the right to a reflective glass elevator mounted on the outside of the building. She went in and remained standing inside with the door open, making no attempt to close it.

Cane went up the steps and saw that her expression did not even change when she saw him. She indicated that he should enter as she inserted a key into the tenth-floor slot. They rode up together in total silence. Exiting, he followed her as she opened apartment 10B's door to a two-bedroom flat. Up to this point, not a word had passed between them. Indicating that he should wait, she entered the bedroom to the right and closed the door. Cane stood there, gazing around at the furniture and furnishings. This was no penny ante apartment. It looked and smell of money.

"Cane, you may come in," he heard a voice said after about fifteen minutes. He entered a dimly exquisitely furnished bedroom, and Jennifer was lying stark naked on black silken sheets. The contrast of such tanned loveliness lying in such a position was too much.

Resistance was futile. He undressed, slipped beside her, and the lovemaking that followed had all the elements of complete gay abandon built in. They panted in unison as they lay sated beside each other. Some time must have passed because he felt a soft blowing in his ears, and since he was waking up, he must have fallen asleep The room was still dimly lit, but the clock on the night stand indicated three a.m.. He had gotten to the Towers just after ten p.m. Jennifer was sitting, still naked, in a lotus position on one side of the huge bed. As he turned around fully, she slapped across his face with all her might. Under alert circumstances, Cane might have been able to duck it, but in his present frame of mind, he got it flush and fell of the bed.

"What the hell is that for?" he exclaimed as he sat upright.

"For letting you back into my life so easy," she said. Those were the first words either of them had uttered from they met, except for the moans and groans during lovemaking.

"After I left you apartment that time," she continued, "I was not feeling well and went back home after completing my nursing status. My worst fears were realized as I discovered that I was pregnant. My parents soon found out also, and when they found out it was for you, a darkie, they kicked me out. I came to London and rented a bedsitter in Fulham. Early in my third trimester, for some reason, which I still don't know, work, cold room, not enough rest, food intake, I had a miscarriage."

Cane was about to say something but she indicated that he should remain quiet.

"Toby, the cafe owner, and his wife were very good to me. After I came out of the hospital and returned to work, he told me about what he thought I should do. Although he would hate losing me, he could see that with my looks, I had loss the weight gained during pregnancy. I was destined for better things. At about the same time, my parents had forward a letter from Charing Cross Hospital stating that I should let them know which starting date from a choice of four would I be interesting to establish my nursing career. But what Toby outlined sounded much more appealing to me at the time. He introduced me to a man who was a manager at 'The Outside Inn,' the most fabulous, elitist nightclub and casino in Soho, London. I was to be groomed, styled, and given a one-bedroom flat in South Kensington. Something like you had in Earls Court. My pay was nothing to write home about, but I would be given a lot of tips acting as a hostess to the single and anyone who wanted someone to talk to. I was never to fraternize with any guest outside of club hours.

"I met Softe about a year ago at the club, and he told me he could get me a job as a model for *London Essence* magazine. The condition was that I would give up this job here and he would put me up in style as long as I was seen with him at least one a week at some ritzy place. There would be no sex involved. I figured it was okay because, at his age, he would probably die if I took him on," she continued, half smiling.

"I later found out that he was gay and had a gay lover, Ivan Kosygin, who was deputy commercial secretary at the Russian Embassy living on the eighteenth floor. He was also part of the arrangement as she went out with him also at least once a week." At first, the tabloids and paparazzi were obnoxious, but after a couple of weeks, they just disappeared, as most times she met Softe downstairs, and the apartment was leased in an offshore company in the Cayman Islands. Their dates were fixed, Softe on Mondays and Ivan of Thursday. On very rare occasion Softe would call her at the last minute because he forgot to line up one of his "ladies" for a particular function he was attending. Ivan preferred to stay in most times, and she would do a strip tease for him while he played with himself. They rarely went out. The lift they came up in was for tenants who did not want to use the main foyer as it was manned by a connoisseur and cameras. Ivan used the underground car park exclusively, and only tenants on his floor might have glimpsed him at any time. Once you inserted your key, and only if you use the outside lift, the lift will only go to that that floor. If you want to go further, there is a phone you call, and the person who answers can adjust from their apartment but your key must remain in the lock. Many movers and shakers in this society live here and quite a large number of foreign personnel. The outside lift is for privacy as one you reach your floor, the opening of the doors automatically turn off the security camera. The security company is still able to, say, if required, who used the lift at any particular time as the key into the slot was recorded digitally. The opening and closing of any door activate or deactivate the security cameras in your vicinity by using the buttons on the key. Continuing, she worked as scheduled demanded it but had a lot of free time and she sometimes traveled for photo opts to the USA and Europe. She was looking over Cane and smiling as she spoke.

"You know," she continued, "that you were the last man I had sex with. Of course, offers were made, but somehow, I never felt able to do so with anyone else, and when I saw you tonight, oh, yes, I saw you." As Cane was about to ask, "I had gotten accustomed to the lighting, and as Softe put on my coat and I spun around, I saw you sitting there, staring. I knew you would follow. Why do you think I hesitated in the lift? I think I would use my vibrator to relieve myself if you had not shown." As she said so, she reached into the nightstand drawer and retrieved a dildo. "I call it my Cane. I have to use it for Ivan sometimes or I would throw it away now that I have the real thing."

Cane got up, relieved himself in the bathroom, and on his return, he saw her looking expectantly at him. Yes, it was his turn to fill in nearly four years of absence. He fingered the amulet ended with the frustration of not finding Mercedes. During breakfast, which Jennifer prepared, the latch at the front door was clicked back, and the door started to open. Cane was alarmed, but looking at Jennifer, she did not even look up. Entering was Jennifer's twin, except that this person was a blue-eyed blonde, while Jenny's hair was dark. Of course, they were not maternal twins, but she was as gorgeous as Jenny. She was introduced to Cane as Sandy Beth Jones. She was Welsh, and her warm embrace told Cane that Jenny had told her about him.

She had the same kind of arrangement, Jenny said, and her men dates were Sundays and Wednesday and also worked as a model for *London Essence Magazine*. One of her clients was Lord Hymn Little, the Queen's cousin; he was also gay, and the other was the managing editor of the *Daily Star* newspaper, Sir Heath Pusey, the Marquis of Romford. He was a bachelor and also loved to be seen with attractive women. He visited often, and Sandy said all she did was to act like a masseuse while naked.

Since it was Tuesday and she had no commitments, they passed the time in the bedroom, filling in gaps of their lives. Sandy had made dinner, and all three of them sat, eating and talking casually. It emerged that Jenny would use all her contacts at every level to find out where Mercedes was, and also, Cane was hooked up with a job at the Outside Inn as a male hostess after Jenny had made several phone calls. A lot of rich, single women frequented that club, Jenny told him.

Back in her bedroom, Jenny told him that she really loved him and he should consider where they would be going in a relationship if for some reason Mercedes had divorced him. If Mercedes was found and everything was okay, she would back away, like she did years ago. The lack of contact with Mercedes was troubling to him, and he had never thought of the possibility of divorce. Who knows what Sir Robert and his cronies might have informed her, that he was missing or killed. Cane was at emotional crossroads. Jenny was willing to give up the "good life" to be with him. He envisaged what working at the Outside Inn and knew that his earnings would be substantial based on what Jenny said when she was there.

Just before he left, Jenny told him that an Under Secretary at the

Ghanian Embassy, Efrim Infume, occupied the flat next to hers. They had glimpsed each from time to time, and on one occasion, she had invited him for coffee. They had chatted about nothing and everything, and she had to feint tiredness and a desire to rest before he finally left after consuming several cups of coffee to her one. A few weeks later, they met in the foyer as she came in, and he invited her for coffee. She accepted, just out of curiosity, and at first, he was an excellent host. The apartment, like hers, was lavishly furnished, and there were pictures of his family, him at his work desk, and various apparent VIPs hung all around talk about his home in Ghana and that he hoped to be the Ghanian ambassador in the near future. She got a bit scared when he began to talk that if she was his wife, she would live like a princess in Ghana as his father was a tribal chief. She felt uneasy, and although she said she had to leave, he was a bit reluctant for her to do so, coming up with all sorts of reason why she should not go just yet. He finally acceded to her request when she threatened that if their encounters were to remain cordial, she would like to leave now, putting emphasis on the now. She had not seen him since that encounter but knew he somehow knew when she was home as her doorbell rang several times, and when she saw who it was through the peephole, did not answer. Cane left late Tuesday night for his own apartment by the outside lift. There was no security going down, just coming up. He had gotten a spare key from Jenny and her phone number, so he knew how to make contact.

The next few weeks flew by, quickly turning into months, and finally into nearly two years. Throughout all this time, he would make enquirers about Mercedes through various channel but to no avail. He finally decided to hire a private detective and gave him all the details about Mercedes and her family in Barbados. A thousand pounds and one month later, the detective, who actually went to Barbados, said he had run into a dead end. For half that amount, he would start a search here in Britain. It was frustrating for Cane who considered the size of Barbados and he came up empty, why would he have better success here, he reasoned. With all things considered, Cane declined the offer. He was not certain how much effort the man had put into finding his quarry as although Braithwaite was a common name, Mr. B was a man of standing and surely someone had to, even at a guess, know something. According to this detective, he drew a blank everywhere. Cane wondered if he just had a wonderful time lazing on golden sand and drinking daquiris.

Cane cut a dashing figure at the club and was very popular. Although black, white women from different nationalities would make very suggestive remarks to him and their willingness to be seduced by him. He would spend Tuesday, Friday, and Saturday nights, rather mornings, after he left work with Jenny if she was not abroad. She never came to his apartment, as although not famous, paparazzi sometimes followed her from photo ops. He had left his phone number and address with the Barbados Embassy, but to date, as he inquired often, there was no info. His little box of phone number papers that he kept was getting quite full. These were from female guests at the club who tipped him very generously, and unfolding, he would see a note with a number and sometimes the time to call. He always mouthed "will try" to them as they left, and days later, another tip with another bit of paper saying, "Try harder."

He showed these to Jenny from time to time and promised her he would never take up any of them. His excuse would be that he was gay; of late, he now found notes from men. They both laughed. Although Jenny never mentioned their relationship as a particular topic, he could sense that she wanted more from him. She was no dodo; her nursing option was still open after all this time. If she quit now from the magazine with what she had saved and his earnings, they could live very well. Even buy a suburban house. Cane promised that once the Mercedes thing was sorted out, they would normalize their relationship. She knew about the private detective and Cane saw how her eyes widened when he told her he had an appointment with a notable law firm to sort out his status as it pertains to marriage.

Plans made by man has no bearing on their eventual destiny, an adage that Cane would come to embrace. It was about four a.m. Wednesday morning. Cane had come from work and let himself up to Jenny's apt. He knew she would be there on a Tuesday night. As he approached her door, it opened, and Ivan stepped out, and at the same Efrim stepped out of his apartment. Sandy was in a see-through dressing gown, and Efrim began to shout in the doorway, and Cane saw that Jenny had appeared also. Probably from the noise that Efrim was making. This scene evolved very quickly. Jenny stepped past Ivan, most likely to confront Efrim who suddenly pulled a gun and approached them. Two shots rang out, and Cane's reaction time was sharp, perhaps a millisecond slower than usual as he had on an overcoat, as he reached Efrim, broke the gun arm as he disarmed, and threw him to the floor. From all the other apartments on that floor, people were emerging in different forms of sleeping attire.

Turning back to Jenny, he was shocked to see her lying on the floor, bleeding profusely. So was Ivan. Cane scooped her up and rushed into the apartment, placing her on the settee as he got towels from the bathroom. He applied pressure to the point of injury, just under her breast, and as her eyes fluttered, tried to reassure her that she would be all right. Sandy had stop screaming, Efrin was moaning loudly on the floor, doubled up in a fetal position, clutching his crotch with his good hand. On the way down to the floor, Cane had cracked his testicles with a stiff chop. The other hand lay limply beside him. It was obvious that Ivan had expired, as a neat bullet hole in his forehead attested to that fact. Either Efrim was a good shot or was just lucky. Based on what he knew of him, it was obvious that he was after Jenny.

Cane had no idea how much time had elapsed as he held Jenny and watched her life ebbed away. He vaguely remembered being roughly pushed aside as he cradled her, and his arms bent behind his back and handcuffs placed on them. What followed after that was lost to his memory. His head and neck ached, so he knew that he was hit in those areas as he slowly tried to focus. When he did, he was in a hospital bed with his right hand chained to the bed. He searched his body for injury, necessitating his hospital admittance, but found none. Looking around, it was a private room as there were no other beds beside him. The memory of what transpired prior to this situation hit him like several two by fours at once. Without knowing why, he started to cry, and as he remembered Jenny, he started to moan loudly. The tears were coming in buckets, and he could not bother to wipe them away as one hand was chained to the bed post. The emotional release that the tears brought weakened his resistance to stay awake. Crying was the last thing he remembered as he drifted off to sleep.

Cane awoke to a very soft calling of his name with a Mister before it. The voice was definitely female, and he turned to the side of the bed from which it came. In view was a very lovely young nurse. She was dressed in the "candy-stripe" uniform, which denotes that she was in training. "My name is Precious Obemfumo, Mr. Cane, and I am not sure if you remember me." Cane tried but could not place this teenager. "I see you still wearing my present," she continued, and all at once her memory came flooding back. He stroked the leather strap tooth that hung around his neck and remembered the softness of the eyes of the little girl who gave it to him. She came around the bed and embraced him. He could only reciprocate with one hand.

Dislodging, she said softly, "I am sorry to see you like this, but I am sure whatever is happening, God will continue to bless you," and she was gone. Cane dozed off again and wondered if he had just had a dream.

"Ah, I see you are awake, Mr. Cane," the voice said as Cane emerged from his slumber. Cane knew that voice; in fact, he would never forget it.

Without turning to the direction of the voice, he said, "What do you want, Sir Morley?" When Cane finally faced him, he could not believe it. He was dressed and looked exactly the same way as Cane saw him nearly four years ago.

Thumbing his fingers together without clasping his hand, he said in his precise upper-class English tone, "Cane, you are one of those persons who are accident prone, but instead of accidents, controversies seems to follow you. I had you under observation from when you visited the Home Office. I must say that I was mildly surprised that you had made it back to England so quickly after the RNA informed that you were demob. To be frank, I had hoped that your endeavor in Nigeria would end in your demise and had no plan B, so to speak, except that your passport was restricted for you to re-enter England. How you did that is neither here nor there; the fact is, you are here now. Of course, you are wondering why am I here after your recent debacle. What happened there was an international fiasco. Had the real story came to light, I doubt Her Majesty's Government would survive. Hence a cover story was put out that you were attempting to force yourself on Ms. Kinner, having gained access to that floor, who screamed, bringing forth other tenants, and in the melee, Mr. Infume, in defending Ms. Kenner, shots were fired, resulting in two fatalities."

Cane could not help himself' he laughed.

Without breaking his monotone, Sir Morley continued, "You are facing a very long term in prison based on the evidence that will be presented against you."

Cane knew that the presence of Sir Morley at his bedside signaled much more than he was he was saying. His mind was clear, and he knew that if he was charged and went to court and lot more than Sir Morley wanted would have to come out. As Cane smiled, Sir Morley said, "Ah, I see that the penny has dropped. Yes, Mr. Cane, to avoid prison, but not the public arrangement that you envisage, I have an assignment for you. You will love this one, as it is in your homeland Jamaica. Once you have signed these papers." He reached into his briefcase and brought out folder. "You will be briefed and put on the first flight to Jamaica." As Sir Morley placed the papers before him, Cane indicated that he was right-handed, and the papers were moved so that he could still signed while chained. Cane signed quickly; he knew for a fact that there was no war or potential war brewing in Jamaica. So what Sir Morley was saying did not make any sense. The signed papers were replaced, and Sir Morley extracted a very thick manila envelope and placed it on the bed and at the same time unbuckled his handcuffs from the bed railing. "Everything you need to know is in this envelope, along with bank drafts and a plane ticket. First class, of course." He rose, and as he reached the door, he said, "Again there is no plan B, but should you return to England, in your absence I will endeavor to find your wife," and he was gone.

In a closet, Cane found his work tux and coat, dressed, and prepared to leave. His watch and other paraphernalia were in a drawer. He was shocked to find out from his date watch that he was sedated for more than a week. Looking through the window, it would appear he was on the top floor of the Charing Cross Hospital private wing.

As he walked towards the lift, he could understand why they would sedate him for a week and keep him incommunicado. Within a couple of days, the story had moved from front page to a column way inside the popular dailies. He later found out, as he relaxed in his apartment, that a court date for his appearance was set later on in the month. Emptying the envelope on his bed, he saw the Jamaican passport, and as he opened it, wondered for a minute who was that person picture staring at him. From the ticket his flight would be eleven-fifty p.m. tomorrow night, getting into Kingston about seven-thirty a.m. He would read the official-looking papers and scrutinize the pictures later. His mind had begun to wander and stopped, with Jennifer in his arms, bleeding, and he began to cry. He wanted to know, how, where Jenny was buried. Were her parents there, what about Sandy? So many questions, but he knew he may never know many of their answers.

The flight was uneventful, and after dinner, he drifted off to sleep. It was a restless sleep as he also dreamt. A cornucopia of events fused into meaningless trivia but featuring the people who had impacted his life so far.

"Mr. Cane...Mr. Cane...You have to be awake for landing." Cane felt a gentle tug on his shoulders and a voice soft and sultry coming from a far distant building, up to a crescendo until it exploded in his brain. He awoke with a start and gazed into a toothpaste ad smile that many an ad agency would pay for. It belonged to Avril Latibeaudiere, the chief purser on the Air Jamaica flight from London-Heathrow to the Norman Manley International in Kingston, Jamaica. As he focused his mind to his surroundings, he was aware that the three other passengers in first class were preparing for landing. They had left London on time at eleven-fifty p.m., and the eight-hour trip put them in Kingston just after eight a.m. The flight, in economy class, was solidly booked, mainly of Jamaicans returning home for holidays. The scarcity of the first-class cabin meant that they did indeed have the "Lovebird Service," as the popular ad say,s from the three attendants in first class including the extremely lovely Ms. Latty, as Cane choose to shorten her name. He smiled as he thought back to Ms. Latty calling him "Mr. Cane," as over the years he had gotten so use to "TAC" by friends and associates alike and was even introduced several times as Mr. TAC. He pulled out his passport to make sure all his paperwork was filled out and gazed at the picture that stared back at him. "Thomas Alexander Cane. DOB: 10/06/40 6,2" tall, with no visible scars," the paged showed. According to the ladies of his life, he was "tall, dark, and handsome." He was eighteen years old when he left, and this was his first return in fifteen years. He had steadily gained a little weight from when he was eighteen at 165 pounds, but over the last ten years had managed to maintain 172 pounds with regular exercise/workouts and a sensible diet. The heavy roar and a thud signaled the lowering of the undercarriage, and TAC looked out the window to see the glistening blue Caribbean Sea beneath the wings. The morning sun on its surface gave it a surreal solid look, and since the approach to touchdown was over water, for a fleeting second the thought would occur that the plane was indeed going to land on it. As he gazed through the window, the sea came rushing up towards him until finally the tarmac came into view, and he felt a gentle bump as the plane touched down and the roar of the retro engines began to slow the plane down. As they taxied towards the gates, Ms. Latty got into her passenger instructions mode. "Please remain seated until the aircraft comes to a stop at the gate and the captain turns off the fasten seatbelt sign." Please do not do this and do not do that etc....and, of course, welcoming all and thanking them for using the services of Air Jamaica and its "lovebird" service.

Jeff McKitty looked into his bathroom mirror and liked what he saw. His distinct walrus mouth stache was his pride and joy. When he spoke, words came out of an office guarded by glistening white teeth. He spoke in a purposeful tone, enunciating every word without sounding halting. At forty-eight, he was also in the peak of health and the youngest head of the Counter Terrorism Unit in the military. Those in the know referred to the unit as CUT, and there were very few people in the know. The unit was set up in 1958, when the first act of terrorism by local and foreign Jamaicans ran the English—who were responsible for defense— ragged as they crisscrossed the island trying to drum up support for their cause, killing a few English soldiers while they did so. The English Administration was caught flat footed as they had no idea who the culprits were. It was the betrayal of the "Liberators," as they were called by local villagers, that finally led to the capture of ten men who terrorized the country for nearly six months. They were quickly tried, and eight faced the hangman; the other two got life sentences.

It was never established whom they were liberating, but it was the consensus at the time that they thought the English should have given up Jamaica to be an independent country. The Jamaican politicians were, it would appear, quite happy at the time for the country to remain under British Rule. Ten years had not elapsed since the incident with the "Liberators," before Jamaica was granted Independence in 1962 from Britain with the stroke of a pen.

CUT was responsible for nipping a communist movement in Jamaica, just after Castro took over Cuba and again during the Cuban Missile Crisis. The Peoples United Party (PUP) and the Labor Party of Jamaica (LPJ) were the two principal political fractions of the independence era. CUT was never disbanded when the local military took over and in fact was responsible for crushing several anti-government military fractions on both sides of the political fence in the last twenty years. The public at large knew very little of these incidents. This info from Sir Robert about Jamaica was news to TAC, as were many other info in the briefings.

A slight cough at the bathroom door established that Jeff's right-hand man, Anthony Drysdale, was standing there, watching his chief grooming himself.

"His plane lands in about forty-five minutes from now, sir," said Anthony.

"That will give us just enough time to get there to welcome him," Jeff replied.

Jeff spoke the word "welcome" in a different tone from the rest of his sentence, and his face hardened as he said so. Whenever they have an assignment of this nature, Jeff and Anthony worked very close, in the sense that they would dine or have breakfast at each other's houses while they worked out strategy. Both their wives and kids over the years left them alone whenever they linked up to plan.

TAC and two men were the first to disembark, and as he entered the terminal building, he looked back to see a vision of loveliness in the person of Ms. Latty standing at the exit door, smiling to the rest of the other passengers. He was the first to reach the Immigration checkpoint and entered the line denoting "Jamaican Passport Holders," as he indeed had a current one. The Immigration officer smiled and welcomed him, taking his documents and entering the data in his computer. A slight pause and change of countenance told TAC that everything was not kosher. Indeed, it was not, as two men materialized beside him, as if they were beamed down by Scotty. It was McKitty and Drysdale. He was invited quite politely to be escorted by them into an annex room. TAC smiled as he walked away, noting that no other passenger had yet entered the Immigration Area except his two traveling companions, and they were occupied in the non-Jamaican line and had not even notice what had happened. As he walked, he could not help wondering what Jamaican Immigration wanted with him.

The room had a desk and a flat table, along with three to four chairs placed in no particular order. Once in the room, nothing was said, except inviting him to sit down with hand gestures....anywhere...and they waited. The wait was not long as, in a short while, the door opened, and his suitcase was brought in a placed on the table. Jeff dismissed the lesser mortals who had brought in the suitcase and turned and to TAC. The briefcase he held was asked for and given, and it was placed on the flat table as well.

"Mr. Cane, the proceedings about to take place will be recorded. Do you have any objections?" said Jeff.

"Objections to what? Feel free to do whatever you have to do, as long as it does not take all morning," TAC replied tersely.

This was not his turf, but years of experience had taught him never allow himself to be intimidated by those who are in control. McKitty fixed him with a stare that would have made any other mortal quiver, but TAC held his gaze until it was McKitty who looked away.

"Kindly open the briefcase and step back," McKitty said.

TAC complied.

All the contents of the briefcase were placed on the table, and each in turn was examined by both men.

Drysdale thumbed through *Our Day Will Come* by Evan Desalle, which TAC had picked up in a London bookstore and told the story of the liberation struggle in Mogadishu, along with *Born Fe Dead* by Elaine Witter, which depicted political corruption, tribalism, and gunmanship in Kingston ghettos, or what the urban sociologists prefer to call "inner cities." Whatever fancy name it was dubbed in those areas, life was different from the mainstream society.

"Interesting reading material you have, Mr. Cane," said Drysdale.

"Perhaps you should read them too. It might improve your perspective as to what is interesting," replied TAC.

TAC saw the backhanded swing of the book and pulled to one side as the book whizzed past his face. McKitty sent daggers of a stare towards Drysdale, and for a moment there was absolute silence. TAC was surprised that Drysdale should react that way to such an innocuous remark and figured that there was more to his detention than meets the eye.

The rest of the interrogation, or rather search of his personal effects, was done in silence as at no time did either McKitty or Drysdale speak to him.

Having replaced everything as they found it, both in his briefcase and suitcase, McKitty asked him to stand up with his arms raised while Drysdale patted him down. While all this was going on, TAC had a half smile on his face and directed to his gaze to whoever's eye he could catch.

"You find this amusing," McKitty said.

"Find what amusing?" TAC replied.

"Our search and questioning."

"Oh, there is questioning to come," TAC said with mock amusement. "I thought you guys were rehearsing for a silent movie or play. I have cooperated with your entire request, and up until now you have not identified yourselves. Inform me why I am singled out and what exactly are you looking for or want." The last part of TAC's sentence was said in a tone which conveyed to those present that he was not going to cooperate very much longer without some answers.

"Oh, I apologize for the inconvenience, Mr. Cane. I am Jeff McKitty, Head of a government bureau," producing a shield as he said so. Drysdale did the same. "Which I am quite sure you are aware—" TAC was about to interrupt, but McKitty waved him silent. "And this is my assistant, Anthony Drysdale."

TAC's smirk returned to his face. He probably knew more about these two than they knew about themselves. He doubted if they knew that they were considered gay by many of their working associates as they spent so much time together. He doubted it.

"The reason for your private search." McKitty raised his hands to indicate parenthesis on the word private. "Is, of course, that your reputation as a troublemaker, inciter, and general subversive activities around the world, especially in third-world countries, preceded you. Not to mention that UNESCO is a bit upset that the project they funded in Zimbabwe to bring fresh water to certain villages that you were overseeing is now dormant since you just up and left, and a considerable amount of money seems to have joined you in that departure." McKitty was enjoying himself, and as he talked, he walked around TAC and emphasized each point with his hands, like a maestro conducting a symphony.

There was long pause, and TAC broke it by saying, "Are you expecting a reply from me?"

"But of course," Mckitty said.

"Okay, TAC said, "listen and listen good. I am a Jamaican citizen traveling on a Jamaican passport. Which I am sure you have verified as genuine by now… based on your whispering to the bearer who returned it a short while ago. I have no contraband in whatever form. You have examined my personal effects, a body search…God knows what you expected to find…perhaps a double-edged sword."

TAC saw Drysdale's faced tighten. "And unless you charge me with something, I am not prepared to answer any questions. If you detain me any longer, I am sure I can get it into the national press….As you say, my reputation preceded me."

McKitty glanced at Drysdale who nodded. "You are free to go, Mr. Cane, and thank you for your cooperation." TAC's little outburst of his "rights" did not cut any ice with McKitty, who was only pushing TAC as far as TAC would let him and would have sent him on his way anytime TAC had demanded it without any threats. At this point, McKitty was not prepared to publicize his department involvement in the return a recalcitrant Jamaican.

As Cane left the office, he knew that a lot of what McKitty had to say was added to his resume by Sir Morley. It covered the period from the end of the war to present day as only MI5 would know his whereabouts in London after he returned. Whatever he hoped to achieve, it would be good for the authorities to know and probably pass on that info to others.

Robert George Dunza poured over the three pages he had just printed from his e-mail. The three concerned three different items, and none of them brought any comfort to his already troubled mind. Here he was the leader of the opposition political party. At sixty-six and had just lost an election that all his lieutenants and the polls assured him that he would have won. He lost, narrowly, but he lost, which meant that he would be in the political wilderness for the next four to five years at least. At seventy/seventy-one, although he was feeling fine now, would be asking his body to do too much. Prior to the elections, he had implemented certain plans in case he lost, and now that he had lost, he had to resurrect them. The assurance from many quarters that he was a winner had caused him to put those plans on ice, but now it was definitely time to thaw them out again. The first report he read was from his contact at the American Embassy, who informed him about the arrival today of one Thomas Alexander Cane. That in itself was not earth shattering because he had taken an interest in TAC ever since he was involved in a coup d'etat which went sour in Abundini, according to his info, and he had to flee for his life. That was two years ago, and his resurfacing in Zimbabwe and winning a UNESCO contract, among many other exploits over the years, was part of the admiration he felt for him. When the country threatened to go Communist in the 1970s under the previous political regime, it was he, Dunda, who, along with CIA aid, stood between democracy and communism. TAC had indicated to him through a third party that he was willing to offer whatever assistance he could to thwart the communist threat. If Fidel Castro was able to get another Caribbean country into the communist camp, it would leave America clout in the region under heavy pressure. The invasion of Grenada a few years later under the guise of protecting American interests and personnel was to make sure that Castro did not get a foothold in that country, as the leader then was anti-American. Dunda's plans were known to four other men who, like himself, were in the political arena, with time running out. The four of them were from Middle Eastern extract, and their parents immigrated to Jamaica several generations ago. Without consultation of each other family, they entered politics at different times; he was the first to do so and built up a strong political following.

When others in his party was losing, they held onto their seats, and when they were winning, they won by huge majorities. It was often said that opponents running against them were just wasting their time. On reflection, it was the parents of these men who had built up influence and economic clout that enabled their sons to enter politics. The indigenous population, at the time of these men's ascension to political power was easily swayed by handouts and bribery. So, unless you had a lot of financial backing, it was difficult to beat one of them at the polls. The Jamaican motto, "out of many one people," adopted in 1962, was a godsend to high brown and white Jamaicans as it legitimized their standing in the society when "Black Power" was the rampant cries of the times. There was always a fair mixture of high brown and white Jamaicans in (HBWJ) both of the predominant political parties, but the majority of high brown white Jamaicans (HBWJ) gravitated to the party which Dunda led. His party consisted of at least six men who were of Middle Eastern extract, and they were permanent fixtures of the party. His association with the CIA was crucial at a time the "communist cry" threatened to sweep the Caribbean. Since that time, he and the resident agent at the US Embassy had developed a rapport. Sometimes he got information before even the government of the day got it. He was very bitter when he lost the election fifteen years ago, and since then, he and his party has been out in the cold. Every election since then, and there were four, his party has lost under his leadership. And each time there was this outcry for him to step down, and each time he managed to remain leader. *But for how much longer?* he asked himself as he turned to the next report he had printed.

This was from the chief geologist of the Canadian firm that was prospecting for gold in the Blue Mountains. A region also famous for his coffee worldwide. The Blue Mountains, according to Melton Zacovich, the chief geologist, was ready to yield gold in a quantity which made it very economically viable, rivaling the yield of any South African gold mine. Dunda frowned; good news and bad. Good for the country, bad for him.

The third report was from Consolidated Oils, which was doing oil and natural gas exploration on the South Coast of the Island. They discovered both, just about three miles offshore, and the early optimism was that both were economically viable for at least the next thirty or so years.

The future portended well for that company, and the country as well. A double economic windfall for the government, which in a short time would get them out of the economic hole they had dug for themselves. This spelled disaster for his political future. If he could not win the last election when the government was unpopular and the country faced economic ruin, how he could ever achieve such a feat with a strong economy and minimal un-employment? The mining and oil exploration ventures would gobble up the vast legions of the unemployed. The domino effect would then generate employment for others. It was a good thing that these reports would not get to the government for another three months at least, and by that time he hoped his plans would bear fruition.

TAC emerged into the brilliant morning sunshine from the arrivals building and made his way to the Avis rent-a-car counter in the rental complex of the airport. McKitty and Drysdale were in the security section, avidly watching the monitor that would pick up TAC when he emerged from Avis. All the rental cars for the various companies were parked parallel fashion, and the camera monitor could easily pick up the license plate of whichever vehicle TAC entered. McKitty was getting a bit anxious. TAC was inside for quite some time now. The next second, he almost lost focus as blood rushed to his head, threatening to create a blackout. Before him on the monitor three, Cane's look-a-like, emerged from the rental center. They slung luggage on the back seat of three Ford Escorts and drove out of the compound in unison. McKitty's breath came sharp and fast; it was only him and Drysdale in one car; no way could they follow three. Why three? Then it hit him. On their way from the airport, the road forks into three at the Harbor View Roundabout. He figured if anyone was following, the cars would each take a different route, making it impossible for any pursuer to know which had the genuine Cane as all the windows of each car was heavily tinted. McKitty's mind raced; he could not call for backup, this operation was an need-to-know basis of his department.

As Cane exited the airport, he saw in his rear-view mirror a 320 BMW overtaking a line of cars, then dropped behind the car behind him. He was in fact in the last of the three lookalike cars. Reaching the three-prong road, one car headed east, the other west, and Cane north. McKitty had decided that he would return to headquarters and wait for things to develop. He was not going on a wild chase. Cane pulled into the Blue Mountain Inn, nestled high up in the country's highest elevation. After registration, he was shown a one-bedroom suite with a fantastic vista of the rolling hills down to the seashore. Standing on the balcony, he inhaled the fresh air, which was intoxicating as it filled his lungs. Relaxing in his room later, he was not sure who or when someone would make contact with him. That contact would be made was certain as, while he was at lunch, his room was professionally searched, and he had no doubt that certain papers were photographed. He knew because he had opened his bottom dresser drawer just a tad, and now it was closed tightly. Without that little occurrence, everything was just as he left it.

After dinner, he decided to go into the capital city to see what the nightlife was about and also to let whoever knows he was here. As he pulled out of the hotel parking lot, he did not let on that he knew he had an uninvited passenger in the rear. The descent was very steep, and the "uninvited" chose to show himself halfway down a steep incline.

"Mr. Cane," he said. "My boss would like to see you, so please follow my instructions." As he spoke, he indicated that he had a gun. Cane smiled, and said, "What if I choose not to follow? Are you going to shoot me? I am certain your boss asked you to come and get me."

The intruder seemed perplexed.

"What with this gun and hiding in the car, you watch too many gangster movies. A knock at my door and your request would be met with a yeah or a nay. Put away your gun, Mr. Gangster, relax, and tell me where you would like me to take you. I am driving, you are in the back seat, so there is nothing you can do to me to prevent us plunging over the ravine should you interfere with me in anyway. Put away the gun and climb over and relax."

The man's face glistened as sweat became aplenty. He swallowed, gulped, and put the gun away and climbed over in the front seat.

"That's better," said Cane. "And your name is...?"

"They call me Shotgun," he finally gulped.

"Well, Mr. Shotgun, where are we off to?" said Cane laughingly.

They traveled through the city, heading west until Cane was instructed to turn off the main road to a secondary road, and as they approached a sign that said, "You are entering Orange Hill. Drive carefully," he was instructed to turn into a lane marked "Private." About a mile down, they came up a gated barrier with a security guard. After chit chat between Mr. Shotgun and the guard, they were waved on. Their destination, as they meandered around sloping bends, seemed to be a house perched atop of a plateau. Throughout their drive, Cane had questioned his passenger as to who is boss was and why he wanted to see him. They only answer he could elicit was that he was a powerful man here in Jamaica and he was only obeying instructions.

It was a huge colonial-type house; a clever investor could easily turn it into a hotel, Cane thought. He was ushered into a sprawling entrance hall and told to wait. After a few minutes, he was ushered into room, where five men were seated around a table with an assortment of liquor glasses and files before them. Cane recognized the five of them from his "manila" envelope as members of Mr. Dunza's opposition cabinet. Mr. Dunza himself sat at the head of the table.

"Welcome, Mr. Cane," he said and invited Cane to sit. Introductions were made, and Dunza got straight to the point. "My colleagues here are not certain about you, and hence I had to give them copies of certain papers that I have privy to and try to convince them that you are the man for the job at hand."

Cane knew that those certain papers were the ones he extracted from his secret compartment, which even McKitty did not find and left them partly secured that they would be found and photographed by the searcher.

"Without you doing anything physical, Mr. Cane, your fee will be five hundred thousand USD, paid into any account you name," Dunza continued. "Of course, the details of what you will be doing cannot be divulged until we have your assurance that you will undertake and the details remain confidential. Once you accept the conditions, you will be moved into this house, and your movements will be restricted for the next two months. After that, you are free to go."

Questions were asked of him by the other four men as they turned leaves from their respective files. In trying to trap him, the same questions were asked differently by another from time to time. In the end, they accepted that Cane was first and foremost a mercenary, without allegiance to any political idea or party. The Thomas Alexander Cane that left Jamaica years ago was not the same person they had in their files.

He was given two days to return with his decision and settle in at the house. Cane was not certain when he would be able to see his grandmother after he accepted this assignment, so as he left Orange Hill, he headed for his grandmother's house near Ochio Rios. He arrived just after midday, and he approached the house; there was no visible change to it after all these years. A young man whom he had not noticed before now ran past him, shouting, "Mrs. Cane, Mrs. Cane, somebody coming to you."

His grandmother appeared on the verandah, and if Cane had not reached her in time, he was sure she was going to collapse as he caught her. She was breathing very heavily, and he sat her in the nearest rocker and waited until she caught her breath. Finally, she just started to stroke his face and called out to someone else in the house. A young lady appeared and was introduced as her "caregiver."

"This is my grandson," she kept repeating as she continued to stroke his face. Cane was finally able to words in edgewise and told her he would come to spend some time with her after he completed some business in Kingston and looked up his dad. She had a phone, so he would let her know when he was coming. She was reluctant to let go of him, but he finally got into car and headed for Kingston.

He was sure he was not followed when he left Orange Hill but did a couple of back-and-forths and noticed the cars around him as he did so. He made a couple of stops en route to his hotel to finalize certain aspects of his future commitment. His main thoughts were focused on how he was going to communicate with others. In two days, he had to overcome that problem. Cane was certain that if and when he left the compound in the ensuing two months, more than likely Mr. Shotgun would stick to him like white on rice. His drop box, for contact, therefore, had to be in Orange Hill. The day before he was due to return, he went to Orange Hill, stopped at the local bar, and bought a couple rounds of drinks to some men who hung out there playing dominoes as they passed the time away. He let it be known that he was a guest of Mr. Dunza and would be here for some time. He was an avid domino player and would love to join in sometime in the future. A chorus of anytime greeted him with the byline, "Loser buys the drinks." Cane nodded his head in agreement and left.

This area was represented by Dunza in parliament and his largess was well known.

When he got up to the house the next day, Dunza, who resided in Kingston at a townhouse during the week, and only return to "the house" on weekends, was furious with him for exposing himself the day before in Orange Hill. Cane pointed out it was better for him to take the initiative by introducing instead of people wondering who he was on catching sight of him in the coming weeks.

"Surely, you have guest here from time to time," Cane argued. "Whatever I will be doing, I am sure it won't be twenty-four seven, so at some point I must have a break. I am also sure that if I am going into Orange Hill, one of your trustees will be with me."

Goings and comings at the "house" were nothing strange to the locals, that's what politicians do, have meetings every chance they get to discuss why they are discussing what to discuss. The "house" was serviced completely by males in every capacity. The cook was very good, as Cane enjoyed all his meals. Dunza, his wife and kids stayed in Kingston, except for Dunda who came down most weekends. The gang of four, as Cane classified them, met that Monday night, with Dunza and himself, and all was revealed. Apparently, a coup d'etat was to be implement as quickly as Cane could work out the dynamics with the information he would be provided with. It was essential that it took place before oil, gas, and gold discovery were announced by the ruling party within ninety days. Cane whistled and ended with a "Wow." All eyes were on him.

"Okay," said Cane, "but you have me in a catch-22 situation. I can't back out now, as I know too much. But I have to have plans, timetables, personnel, movements, and a whole lot of logistic information before I could even contemplate what you are asking…."

Dunza smiled and opened a six-drawer file cabinet situated in the far corner of the room. "Mr. Cane, this was our plan B for some time, so within this cabinet you will find all you need. Once you are comfortable with our plans and information, let me know if there is anything you will need extra."

The meeting was terminated, and Cane said he would start bright and early in the morning. As he replaced the one set of files into the top drawer, he noticed a Smith and Weston six-shooter at the bottom of the drawer. He wondered what it was for.

Cane was really surprised how well organized Dunza was. His initial going over of the maps, charts, files, and other pertinent information revealed a thorough and comprehensive collection of data. After categorizing the different aspects of how the coup would be implemented, he decided to take a break after three days. The bar had a few men, and Cane ordered drinks for everyone and asked about the domino game. There was a reluctance at first because, since it was Thursday, and money was tight, no one wanted to take on a game where they would have to buy if they lost the set of six. Cane assured them that when he won, not if, they could owe him until the next time. They all laughed at the "when he won" part, and pretty soon the game was going. Cane knew dominoes well, and so at any point where he was winning, he would make a bad play, ensuring that their opponents would win the set. Of course it would be Cane paying the bar bill each time. This scenario continued for the next three weeks, with Cane working on papers until late most nights and going to the bar on Thursdays. Shotgun reported to Dunza that everything was kosher, and Dunza himself was pleased at the progress being made.

Cane informed Dunza that he would be presenting the final draft of what would be taking place with just a few areas to fine tune the following weekend, including the date. Dunza was static, could hardly contain himself as he gushed to his fellow coupers. They had to hush him from time to time as he was appearing to raise his voice a bit too much for their comfort. They kept nodding and told him, "Weekend…weekend."

With all eyes and gazing with rapt attention, Cane began his oratory in front of his charts. "Gentlemen," he began, "first of all, let's get rid of the notion that a coup in any country must be carried out by the army with a show of force. Not necessarily. With coordinated planning, a few can do it, and this is what will happen. There are seven key areas to overcome: The army barracks situated East, West, Central, and in the city; the two radio stations and the TV station." In answer to a question about police stations, he said that they are not critical as none of them would have the fire or manpower to overcome an army unit if they chose not to accede to the new order. The four politicians there represent the areas where the army barracks are situated, and they would lead from the front in coordinating the final movement. Cane went over several times each chart until they could conduct the meeting as if they were the leader. After he was certain that everything was nailed down, including Dunda's assurance that he would get seven powerful all-island coverage walkie-talkies, Cane prepared for the coup de gras...the timing of the coup.

Cane flipped over the last remaining chart. "Monday the fourth of October, just over a week away, is designated a local holiday; everything is shut down. "That means," he continued, "we will act on the night of the third, Sunday night at four a.m., in fact Monday morning. The time is crucial as before guard change at six a.m., traffic drops to almost zero, and guards are sleepy. With everything in place, the populous won't know what had happen until possible Tuesday. If, and it is a big if, something catastrophic happens to make that date impossible, then we go to plan B." He looked around to Dunza and smiled. "The following weekend. On the day of the third, based on what we have gone over, it is still a go if something happens, like an earthquake, four hours before zero hour. With four hours to go, nothing can stop unless an act of God, to which I have no control. From what you have seen and the knowledge you now have, is there anything any one of you cannot comprehend to take to your own lieutenants?"

The consensus was nothing.

That Thursday night, Shotgun was not a very good domino partner, and they lost almost every set. With those little numbers before him and the bigger picture in his mind, it was difficult for him to concentrate. Cane kept paying the bills as losers gladly. Normally, he would not position himself to see what Cane was doing, as he paid the bills, but for some reason, he got up just as Cane placed a twenty-dollar-bill on the counter and slid it to the bartender. Shotgun took up the bill and felt the other piece of paper underneath before Cane could react. He indicated to Cane that he was carrying by tapping his waist and nodded for them to leave. Cane knew that at this point if he tried anything, Shotgun would indeed shoot, and the innocent might be injured.

Cane was driving, and as they stopped at the house, Shotgun jumped out and covered him with the gun, indicating for him to go to his room. He heard the lock click and the removal of the key as he entered. That door was the only way in or out of this room. Cane knew exactly what Shotgun was going to do once he read the note he had slipped under the twenty-dollar bill. It would take about two hours before anything happened, so he showered and watched TV quite calmly. It was two days before zero hour.

Right on cue, the door opened and in stormed Dunza with the note and a German X4 Luger in his hand. He was literally foaming at the mouth. Behind him was Shotgun, also gun in hand. He was ushered into the large meeting room where the other gang members were. Recriminations came from Benhassim who said he had his doubts from the beginning about trusting Cane. Dunza signaled for silence and read out the note Shotgun had given him.

To BIN
From- TAC – joint Sanhhurst 1
Coup will take place on OCT. 11 at 001 am by Dunza crew hitting aforementioned sites. Do not initiate any troop movement before said time so as not to arouse suspicion by any pro-Dunza army personnel.

As Dunza read, Cane's thoughts were elsewhere. The note was written on a piece of paper the same size as a twenty-dollar-bill, and Cane wondered how Shotgun saw it, as he was very careful, as in previous times, in handing info to the barkeep who was his contact. "Well," shouted Dunza, "what do you have to say?"

Cane got up slowly, and six guns were leveled at him. "You are missing the point," he began. "Of course I am an army plant, initially, but as you strongly pointed out at our first meeting, I have no allegiance to anyone or anything, only to money. I did all this planning to a fine point. The army expected something, so I gave them something, based on previous info. When I considered the successful outcome of this planning, I needed to be around and enjoy the good life before leaving. The good life, which I am sure you would extend to me, apart from the money already in my account. So, I had to make sure that I satisfied both parties. Look at the date and time of my note; it's eight days after you had already taken over. The army would be planning for a coup a week after it would have happened. Once you were in charge and probably learned of my note warning, the army the outcome would be the same." For the first time, they all converged on the note to check the date. A lot of nodding and shaking of head followed, and after about ten minutes was ordered to sit. Finally, it was agreed that Cane should send the note. Benhassen asked why the time on the note was written with 00 before, and Cane explained that all over the world, time is written with 00, so as to be precise and no misunderstanding between a.m. and p.m., 13:00 would be one p.m. in the afternoon, while 001 would be one a.m. in the morning. He was about to ask another question but saw that his fellow plotters were nodding, accepting that explaination. The next afternoon, he and Shotgun went to the bar; it was early, so the usual bar patrons were not there yet. Cane told the barman he was just passing through and asked him to change a twenty for two tens. He obliged, and they left. The note was passed.

Shotgun returned him to the meeting room. For the first time he noticed a Gruman X706 walkie talkie receiver with seven blinking green lights, very little static emanating from it, sitting on a table in the far corner. Earlier, Cane had seen workmen putting something on the roof. Dunza must have brought the equipment when he came earlier.

"Okay, Cane," began Dunda, "we accept your explanation, but to satisfy any qualms we may have, you will be in this room from now until the coup. Gatorfoot"—apparently all these men had aliases, as he indicated a sour-looking man—"and myself will be with you until zero time. You will be monitoring the communications and addressing any flaws that might crop up. All the necessary amenities are through that door." He indicated a door to his left. "And your food will be brought in as requested. Your clothes and toiletries will be transferred over."

Short-wave radio transmissions can be picked up by anyone who happens at the precise moment to get on the right frequency. The Gruman had alternating frequency modulator, which made it very difficult for a non-accredited person to lock onto.

Zero hour was thirty minutes away. Cane began to call, "Apple One… this is Papa. What is your status, over?"

"Twenty-nine and counting with everything a-okay, over," came the reply.

"Baker One, this Papa. What is your status?"

"Twenty-eight and counting with everything a-okay, over." Charlie One was Benhassem, his doubter, and he sounded confident and assured as he replied. When Cane had finished all his calling, he indicated to Dunza and Gatorfoot where on the charts the units were. They were ten minutes from zero hour. After zero hour it would take between five to fifteen minutes for reports to filter back that everything had gone as planned. Cane assured Dunza that those would be the most anxious minutes, but so far, there was 99.99 percent for optimism.

As soon as the radio stations were taken and controlled, the apparatus was set up for Dunza to broadcast to the nation what had taken place. The radio stations were assigned to Charlie and Easy units. Five minutes after zero-hour, Charlie unit called in…. Mission accomplished; this was followed by Easy company with the same message.

Dunza was in his element; his recorded tape was broadcasting to the whole of Jamaica from the radio stations his men had just taken over. His smile broadened as he listened to himself denouncing the government and the bountiful and glorious days that were forthcoming under his leadership. Dunza was stroking his chin and smiling as he listened; a frown was appearing on Gatorfoot's face, as none of the other units had called. Twenty minutes later, Dunza was running when he became apprehensive why the other units had not called in. Cane said it could be a technical glitch and tried to raise them.

"Police…police…army…soldiers…soldiers," came a shouting voice over the guard gate intercom into the room, followed by gunshots. Gatorfoot pulled his gun and hustled out. Dunza stood there, looking at Cane as more shots rang out nearer to the house. It finally dawned on him that something had hopelessly gone wrong, and he reached into his jacket for his Luger. As his first shot rang out, Cane dived behind one of the huge chairs at the end of the table. He had managed to retrieve the six-shooter from the cabinet and returned fire as Dunza took cover also. Dunza knew he had to finish this quickly as shouts and firing were getting closer, and he had to get away. Cane and himself were exchanging gunfire, when he heard the hammer of Cane's gun hitting an empty chamber. Two more *clack...clack*. Dunza called Cane to come out and face him like a man and stepped from behind his cover. Cane obliged, and they stood face to face.

"How did you do it?" Dunza asked in anguish.

"Binary, binary," replied Cane.

"Bine what?" said Dunza as he raised his gun, taking aim at Cane who still held his six-shooter in his hand.

Cane couldn't remember the millisecond before Dunza saw the flask from six-shooter nozzle if his expression changed. The bullet hit him flush in the forehead, and a glazed look came into his eyes before he crashed to the ground dead. At the same time, the door burst open, with David Black leading the charge. In the aftermath that followed, members of Dunza party said they were shocked at what happened, and general aspersions were cast on the party. Cane knew that if the coup was accomplished, many of the deniers would have gladly accept cabinet positions in the Dunza government.

Cane, David, and his wife Sharon were sitting by the pool side of the Intercontinental Hotel in Kingston, sipping margaritas.

"When I saw the note," said David, and it was different from the others, I had to take stock. First, the 'to' initials were wrong, and then the Sandhurst joint thing. Well, once I worked that out, it was simple. Yes, we were joint in computer studies. You said Dunza stared at you when you said binary, he had to, how many folks know that digital computers operate on two numbers, zero and one. Zero is off and one is on, for the electronic grid numbers, hence one, one in Binary is three and zero, zero, one is four...."

"I don't understand," chimed his wife.

"I will show you later," said David.

"Show her now," said Cane, smiling.

"Okay. Imagine a grid with the numbers one, two, four, eight, sixteen, thirty-two, all the way into the thousands. You will notice the numbers keep doubling all the time. Well, suppose I wanted to write twenty, it would look like this—00101… You see, zero under one and two, And one under the four, zero under the eight, and a one under the sixteen. So only the numbers that have a one is the right number, and those add up to twenty. Sixteen plus four."

After some more explanations, Sharon got it. They were about to leave, when David asked how did he manage to shoot Dunza so face to face. Cane said that he knew Dunza had another clip for his Luger and would, in the end, outshoot him when there was no reply from him. To draw him out, he manually turned the chamber around until he was on the fourth chamber. By clicking twice, fourth, and fifth, he was now on the sixth, which was live. Dunza thought his gun was empty stood up and confronted him. It was better that way, said David, because the whole of Jamaica heard his ramblings. By allowing his men to "capture" the radio stations, there would be no doubt in anyone mind what took place.

After about two weeks, the buzz had died down and comments could be found on the back inside page of the dailies. McKitty wondered how military intelligence had gotten the scoop about Cane. Not being able to find him after that first day had annoyed him considerably. After an informer had told him about the stranger in Orange Hill from England, he was about to act, when a note from the head of the Military Intelligence Unit told him to lay off. They were on the same side, so he felt okay with the outcome.

Cane opened the letter at about thirty thousand feet on the BOAC flight to London from Kingston. It was handed to him by the Purser about a half hour into the flight. From the official seal on the outside, Cane knew who it was from. The Prime Minister expressed his gratitude for his role in the abortive coup and hope Cane would live long and prosper. Cane was at his grandmother's house, and after assuring her that he was okay, except for Mercedes, her blood pressure and all other highlighted levels because of seeing her grandson alive again returned to normal. His father, now prime minister, had visited, without fanfare as usual. After his mom died and he went to live with his mother-mother, his father entered politics, and as the years passed, he rose in stature within his party. He entered as a single man, never got married nor was associated with any particular female but with many. No one associated Thomas as the son of the prime minister. Cane can't remember if there is even a picture of them together. There was no animosity or ill feeling;

he was just his dad. Cane knew what love is because the same in depth aching he felt for his grandmother at times was the same he felt for Mercedes. He folded the letter and fell into a blissful sleep, awakened only when the plane was about to touch down at Heathrow Airport.

He was about to exit the terminal building after clearing Immigration and Customs when an official-looking lady in some sort of uniform called him by name and requested that he followed her. He was shown into a room with desk and chairs and asked to be seated. Whatever was going on, Cane thought, Sir Morley had something to do with it. The door opened, and a boy of his own coloring about six or seven entered and said, "Are you my daddy?" Cane was flabbergasted. Before he could collect his thoughts, a little girl, easily the boy's sister and probably twin, entered as well. Now is flabber was gasted. The door opened wider, and there, standing in all her glory, was Mercedes.

He stared, his mouth opened. He tried to move but felt paralyzed. The woman before him was his Mercedes. If she was these children's mother, motherhood had enhanced her beauty and structure. Time was not her enemy but a tremendous ally. She raised her arms in welcome, and Cane felt the surge of blood flow as every fiber of his being became alive and started to tingle. They hugged, not searching for each other's lips but just in a tight embrace. His body shivered, and he began to cry softly and uncontrollably. He remembered the last time this happened to him. The tears came down in torrents, soaking her coat where his face rested on her shoulder.

"Mommy, why are you crying?" he heard the little girl ask. He regained his composure and pulled slightly away. He saw the tears on her face and kissed them softly, as the kids make yucky sounds.

She pulled away. "Andre and Andrea, meet your daddy." Cane hugged both of them together, and for a first-time meeting, they hugged him back.

In the provided car driving away from the airport, each child was busy challenging each other who could tell the most outrageous story to Daddy. After about half an hour, they fell asleep in Cane's and Mercedes's arms. After about an hour, they arrived at a detached townhouse at a place called Hounslow New Town. Cane, alighted, could see that there were still a lot of construction going on as there were workmen putting finishing touches on quite a number of houses. The kids were now awake, and as they approached the porch the door opened, it could only be Mercedes's mother who stood there. Right again, as the kids rushed to her shouting, Grandma, Grandma, Daddy is here." This was the first time he was seeing her in person.

"I am certain," he said, "that when you go out with the kids and they are heard calling you Grandma, a lot of heads turn, as most would have figured you are their mom."

Mrs. Braithwaite's expression did not change for a few seconds, then she embraced Cane and whispered, "I see why Mercedes is married to you, you are quite a charmer." Cane thought if Mercedes looked like this at her age, then he was indeed a fortunate man, because Mrs. B was still stunningly attractive. After lunch, the kids showed him every piece of toy they possessed, and they went off for a nap.

Sitting on the back porch feeling a different type of tranquility, Cane held his wife's hand as he unfolded the missing time from her. He held nothing back and felt the pressure of her hand increased when he had reached to point of Jennifer" death. He began to shake his head when he thought of the years back from Lagos and he was not more than forty miles from her. She in turn told him that returning from the airport, she had called her parents, and her dad arrived the next day. He wanted to get her away from Earls Court, in case there could be repercussions from some nut job who knew she was his wife. Hounslow New Town was under construction, and what it offered in terms of what the developers wanted suited her ideally. Basically, they wanted a multi-ethnic township with young, married professionals. As he can see they are still building, although there were some six hundred married couples with families already here. Many granddads and grandmas, spinster sister, bachelor brother made up many family units. It was not just young people, although they were in the majority. Her dad had contacts and got a finished one almost immediately No sooner had they moved in, she discovered that she was pregnant. She kept in touch with her three main friends by phone only. Her dad said until such time that Cane was deceased, he thought that she would be in some danger from zealots. She had missed a few days of the pill, due to the excitement of becoming a Misses, she laughed. Her mom came up and has been with her ever since. Dad popped in every Christmas and some other odd times.

Most of the female side of her family had twins, so she was not surprised when the doctor told her that was the case. As long as she was able, because she wanted to, she worked mainly the day shift at the General Hospital about twenty-five minutes away. She did not even remember that she had a joint account with him.

"A few days ago," she continued, "A man came to the house and said that he was from the British Home Office. His credentials seemed in order, and he explained that you were alive and would be coming to London early next week. Cane, I believe that I went into cardiac arrest. The man was looking at me funny and kept asking if I was all right. He finally called my mom to bring a glass of water. She was anxious to know what was happening, and on hearing the news, we just hugged and cried. The Home Office man must have wondered if he was in a house with nutty females. My heart began to race even faster when he said that you would be coming in from Jamaica. I could not fathom how Lagos became Jamaica. It would not have matter if he said you were descending from heaven, the fact that you would be here was enough to lift the ache that stayed with me from the day you left. A car would be sent to pick us up at the appointed time." Her face was close to his, and the kiss finally came. It was very long; two people were exchanging auras, and it took time. The animalistic fervor that usual go with such physical contact was absent. Instead, there was a condescending promise of the unification of bodies at a later time. As they broke apart and stared into each other eyes, the looks said, "….I am going to love you ravenously later."

Later that night, after putting his children to bed on their insistence, he lay waiting for his wife to join him. Sir Morley had kept his promise and found his wife for him. Knowing Sir Morley Cane wondered if he knew all along her whereabouts. There was no doubt in his mind that the unison with his wife tonight would surpass all others because he felt the absolute oneness when he held her after so many years at the airport and, later, on the back porch as they kissed. He was brought up in the Church by his grandmother and attended church often before leaving Jamaica. As he grew older, he had drifted away as circumstances engulfed him. Reflecting on his life she knew that what had happened to him so far was not typical. He now had a son and a daughter to whom he would dedicate the rest of his life in bringing happiness to them. He turned to see his wife silhouetted at the bathroom door and knew he had to give thanks to someone or something superior to his being for the bounty he now possessed.